GUT-CHECKED

MESSY HEARTS #3

CHARITY PARKERSON

—Warning: This book is intended for readers over the age of 18.

Copyright © 2020 Charity Parkerson
Editor: Hercules Editing & Consultants
ISBN: 978-1-946099-68-6
All rights reserved.

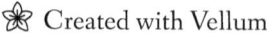 Created with Vellum

Cruz thought they were perfect. Ford couldn't take the loneliness any longer. Everything will need to change to save them.

Ford has been Cruz's best friend for a few years. Their friends-with-benefits arrangement has always worked for Cruz. Cruz isn't seeing anyone else. He assumes Ford is the same. It's a perfect relationship as far as Cruz is concerned. He's too busy running his successful custom bike shop to look too closely at their relationship. Then it's gone.

Since Ford met Cruz, he's been in love. Despite Cruz's inability to see anything beyond his success,

Cruz is still pretty amazing. He's gorgeous and fun. He's that guy who never loses. The problem is, Cruz doesn't love Ford. He could walk away anytime, and Ford wants someone who can't live without him. Ford knows there's no way he'll ever have a normal life with Cruz, and as long as he stays close by, he'll never stop saying yes when Cruz calls. That's why he takes a job over three hundred miles away from the man who owns his heart. It's the only way he'll ever be free.

When Ford drops the news that's he's done and moving away, Cruz has to find a way to stop him. Everything he believed about their relationship has to change. While Cruz has no intention of letting Ford get away, this might be the one time he doesn't get his way.

ONE

Cruz: *I FUCKED UP TONIGHT, SURPRISING NO ONE.*

Cruz paused and thought over that statement and decided to add a caveat.

Cruz: *Well, I'm sure it shocked the hell out of Raiden when I punched him in the face.*

Three little dots jumped and danced on Cruz's phone, showing Ford was typing. Cruz drew a steady breath, waiting to hear the response from the only person whose opinion really mattered. This was the only time of day when he felt truly relaxed.

Ford: *Raiden? The guy dating Jason? That Raiden?*

Cruz: *That's the one.*

The phone rang in Cruz's hand. Cruz bit back a smile as he answered. "Hello?"

"Why did you hit Raiden?" Ford asked, not bothering to say hello.

"It's a long story where I was wrong, as usual. Tell me about your night instead. It had to have been better than mine."

Ford never hesitated to give him exactly what he wanted. This time was no exception. "It went. I watched some TV, ate, and breathed. Now answer my question."

Cruz tilted his chin up and stared at the ceiling. "You weren't there to be my good sense."

A snort sounded through the line. "You know damn well no one can be your good sense."

"Mhmm." The hum vibrated in Cruz's throat without thought. He kicked back in his recliner and closed his eyes. An image of Ford waited for him there. Brown hair that was always a mess and dark blue eyes that always flashed with caution were only the vaguest descriptions of Ford. There were no words to do him justice. Ford had something that came from the inside. This mysterious trait poured out when Cruz stood in his presence. He made Cruz feel... everything, in truth. Powerful and wanted. Elated and ridiculous. Angry and frustrated.

"Come see me."

Ford didn't answer right away. When he did, he

sounded cautious. "Well, I was kind of already in for the night."

"Please?" Cruz wasn't above begging Ford. No one else ever heard him plead for attention. "We could play some pool, crank up the music, and drink. You can have fun without having to deal with a crowded bar. I know how much you hate those."

Once again, silence met his offer. Finally, Ford cleared his throat. "Why don't you come see me instead?"

"I've been drinking." He hadn't. "You know I don't drink and drive."

"Maybe some other time, then," Ford said, as if the matter was settled.

Cruz bit back a growl. "Fine. I'll come to you."

"I'd rather you didn't." Ford sounded every bit as aggravated as Cruz. "You said you've been drinking, so you shouldn't be driving. Just go to bed and maybe I'll see you tomorrow."

An evil smile pulled at Cruz's lips. "If you don't want me driving, come see me."

"No."

Damn. Ford had zero hesitation in his voice. Cruz hated that. "I miss you, Ford. Are you really refusing to come see your best friend in his time of need? I got in a fight tonight."

A sexy growl caressed his ear. "You know as well as I do that you'll call the next guy on your list when you're done talking to me. If he says no, you'll call the next and then the next until someone says yes. You won't think about me at all after our call."

Cruz's chest hurt. He fucking hated that Ford believed that. "That's not true. I'll be there in twenty."

"Goddamn it, Cruz. Do not drink and drive."

"Then come see me. I'm seeing you tonight one way or the other." Ford didn't respond. Cruz tried waiting him out. Ford didn't budge. Cruz flinched first. "I'll tell you the whole story about hitting Raiden if you come."

"Goddamn it. I'll be there in thirty minutes, you fucking bastard."

It was hard, but Cruz tried not to sound triumphant. "Okay. I'll keep an eye out for you."

Ford hung up without saying goodbye. Cruz wasn't upset. He set the phone aside, crossed his arms over his chest, his feet at the ankles, and settled in to wait. Cruz tried not to think about Ford's accusation. He wasn't sure why Ford believed Cruz had a long list of men on speed dial. Cruz didn't have time for that type of distraction. For as long as he could recall, Iconic Stylin' Rides had been his only

4

dream. His everything. Cruz had done a lot to make that dream come true. He wouldn't stop wheeling and dealing, because he needed to ensure the shop stayed profitable. Having a list of men on his phone took energy Cruz didn't have to expend. Plus, he already had Ford. Cruz didn't need anyone else. Ford was Cruz's best friend. His confidant. Cruz's chest tightened. Ford was Cruz's reason for everything. There was no one elsc. He had no fucking clue why Ford refused to see it. Maybe it was time for a few confessions.

EVEN AS FORD STRADDLED HIS HARLEY, HE couldn't fucking believe he was doing this. Goddamn Cruz. He always manipulated Ford into getting out of bed, driving to his place, and regretting his life decisions. But damn, Cruz was beautiful. Like, supermodel, famous actor, and rock star gorgeous all wrapped into one. He turned heads and stunned people into silence. Topping all that, he was nice and funny. Likable. Cruz absolutely fucked with people's heads. He made them feel wanted. Cruz made people feel seen. He was a goddamn wrecking ball because Cruz didn't really see anything beyond his motorcycle shop. What Cruz did was an art, designing the perfect customizations, and Cruz was completely addicted to working. Everything else in his life was squeezed in during his short bursts of boredom. As his best friend, Ford fell under the "everything" umbrella. He would never be as important as he would like.

At least five times before making it to Cruz's place, Ford almost turned around and went back home. The thing was, though, Cruz was Ford's best friend. If he called, Cruz would come. Ford would do the same. He couldn't deny Cruz anything. Truthfully, it was a bit pathetic and Ford was one hundred percent self-aware.

Cruz's massive house came into view. Ford still didn't understand how two such opposites had become so close over the past three years. Even though no one could look at Cruz and tell he had mad money, Ford still felt weird every time he visited Cruz. He felt like a pity friend. Ford parked close to the front door and jogged up the steps. He wouldn't stay long. The too-wide front door swung open before Ford reached it. Cruz stood on the other side, looking like a sexy god.

"Hey, gorgeous."

Ford nearly snorted at the greeting. "I'm here. Tell me the Raiden story."

Cruz's mouth lifted in one corner. Ford had to take a slow breath. Cruz's eyes flashed with heat as he closed the door and the distance between them. "I said I'd tell you after you come. You haven't come yet." He reached for Ford, going straight for the button of Ford's jeans.

Ford took a step back out of his reach. "I guess I'm not hearing the story then."

The way Cruz chuckled said he wasn't offended. "Come on. There's a drink and pool stick with your name on them."

That was all Ford needed to hear. He headed for Cruz's playroom. Ford had been to this house countless times. He knew every inch of the place. Cruz probably would let Ford move in anytime he wanted. All Ford had to do was say he needed Cruz. The thing was, Ford didn't want to need Cruz while Cruz—no doubt—fucked anyone who said yes. While Ford had never actually seen Cruz with anyone else, he knew in his heart someone as beautiful as Cruz was beating people off with a stick. No way was he turning down any ass, and Cruz didn't make much time for Ford these days. Ford cleared the doorway of Cruz's man cave. He skirted the pool table and headed for the bar.

He turned as he reached the first barstool. "Since I'm here, I really need to talk—" Cruz's body collided with Ford's, trapping him against the bar and cutting off his words. Before Ford could protest, Cruz's mouth covered his. Ford wanted to push him away. In fact, his hands flattened against Cruz's chest. A whimper reverberated off the walls of his brain at the hardness of Cruz's muscles beneath his hands. His fingers caressed rather than shoving. He found himself sucking Cruz's bottom lip. His stomach cramped with desire. Not for sex. Ford craved being wanted for real. He wished he wasn't a weak booty call who came running whenever Cruz crooked his finger. Yeah, he was Cruz's friend, but that was all he would ever be, and it wasn't enough. That thought gave him the strength to push Cruz away.

"That's enough. I really need to tell you something."

Cruz dropped to his knees.

Ford dropped his gaze.

While holding his stare, Cruz popped the button on Ford's jeans. "Tell me when my lips are wrapped around your cock... if you can still speak," Cruz dared.

Ford broke. "I'm moving to Phoenix."

Cruz froze. Without breaking eye contact, Cruz pushed to his feet. He moved closer. There wasn't a strip of light between them as Cruz eyed Ford. His features grew harder by the second. "What's in Phoenix?"

"A job."

Still, Cruz's expression gave nothing away. "A job."

"A better job," Ford said, incapable of not expounding in the face of the growing tension.

"There's a position open at the shop. I told Raiden I would hold it for him, but he won't take it. It's yours. I'll pay you whatever you need to stay."

Ford hadn't wanted it to come to this. He hadn't wanted to explain his reasons for leaving. Ford had truly hoped he could just quietly go. "There's something else waiting in Phoenix that I need."

"What?" The way Cruz barked the question made Ford jump.

"Space away from you."

Something settled in Cruz's eyes. It tightened Ford's chest and grew between them. "What's that supposed to mean?"

Ford took a deep breath. He hated everything about this, but it was well past the time he should have spoken up and saved his heart from further damage. "It means I don't want to be just a number in someone's phone anymore. I don't want to get dressed at nearly midnight to drive across town for someone who never does the same for me. If I stay, my life will be like this forever. Maybe, in Phoenix, I'll meet someone who wants to grow old and fat with me." Despite the horrible situation, a small smile touched Ford's lips at the thought. He really wanted to grow old and fat with someone who loved him.

Cruz visibly swallowed—like his throat had rapidly swelled. "You're not just a number in my phone."

The backs of Ford's eyes burned. The sensation pissed him off. He was tired of silently hurting and longing for someone who did not feel the same. "Three years, Cruz. I've been doing this with you for three years. Has it ever occurred to you that I might want to mean more to someone? Three. Years."

A deep line appeared between Cruz's eyebrows. "Mean more than what? I've told you a thousand goddamn times that I don't call anyone else. If you tell me no, then it's no and I go to bed alone. I'm not seeing anyone else. Hell, you could move your things in tomorrow, and we'll get fat. I don't give a shit.

There's a job at the shop if you need more money than you're currently making. Better yet, I can take care of you. Quit and spend your days with me while I work. There's not a goddamn thing in Phoenix for you. It's right here. With me."

Ford heard Cruz. He really did, but it was all bullshit. Oh, he knew he could move his things in tomorrow. He could accept Cruz's job or let Cruz take care of him, but Cruz didn't really mean anything he said. There was a big difference between actions and feelings. If Cruz felt Ford, he wouldn't be half-ass making these offers now. He would have shown up after work every night for the past three years. Taken him to dinner. Cruz would have been fucking normal. But Cruz hadn't done any of those things. Ford didn't really matter at all and it would slowly kill him if he stayed.

Ford wished this part didn't hurt so much. "You'll always be my best friend."

Cruz huffed. "But you're still going. Is that what you're saying?"

"I've given you time. This isn't me threatening to leave so I'll get my way. If you really wanted to be with me, nothing would've stopped you. I wouldn't have needed to point out that we aren't real, because you never would've let me doubt us. This," Ford said, sounding desperate even to his ears as he motioned between them. "This is just playtime to you. I'm just some guy you fuck when you get bored. I'm getting too old for this, Cruz." Against his better judgment, Ford's hands slid across Cruz's hips. He couldn't help but touch Cruz one more time. "You'll see once I'm gone. Everything will be fine. I imagine you won't think about me at all." Damn. That hurt, because Ford one hundred percent knew it was the truth.

"When are you leaving?"

"June first."

Cruz's eyes lit. "So I still have two months with you."

Ford hated everything about this. He shook his head. "I don't think so, baby. It's best if we say our goodbyes now. I have a lot to take care of over the next few weeks. I won't be coming back here." Ford pushed away from the bar, leaving Cruz no choice but to take a step back. He tried stepping around him.

Cruz shifted sideways, blocking his path. "Don't go just yet. At least kiss me one last time."

There was no way Ford could say no. He knew he shouldn't give in, but it would be for the last time. Ford's hands slid across Cruz's hips again. They kept going without his permission until Ford cupped Cruz's firm ass. He massaged even as he drew Cruz closer. Cruz's face flushed. His lips parted on a breath. Everything slipped away but the man he held. Cruz would never know the cost of this moment. From the first time they kissed, Ford had been ruined for anyone else. He was completely in love with Cruz. Ford loved someone who would never love him back. He captured Cruz's lips. Ford's knees weakened. Cruz kissed the same way he sucked dick—slow and methodical. Sometimes, for just a moment, Cruz's kiss would trick Ford into thinking Cruz felt the same. Then the next day would bring reality back like a speeding train.

Ford stroked Cruz's ass and back. He rubbed Cruz's sides and then stroked his chest. His hands found Cruz's face and held on. His fingers savored the sensation of Cruz's jaw working as he poured his heart into their kiss. Ford pulled away and pressed his forehead to Cruz's. With his eyes squeezed shut, Ford mentally snipped the ties that held him to Cruz. He was giving up a dream he had for himself for three years by walking away from Cruz. But, at some point, this had become a hell of his making. So he would stop.

Ford tore his hands away from Cruz's face and

walked away. He didn't look back. Even as he jogged down the front steps and headed for his bike, and his mind screamed for him to take one last peek at the life he had wanted so goddamn badly, Ford didn't slow. They were done. It was over.

TWO

TIME PASSED WITHOUT FORD. CRUZ DRANK AND then drank some more. The sun came up and went down again. Cruz thought he might have passed out a little in between, but he was too drunk to tell. He didn't text Ford, and it was like quitting drugs cold turkey. For three years, he had texted Ford every single day with every random thought. Now there was nothing but the memory of him left to sustain Cruz.

Cruz could still recall the first time he saw Ford. He had bought an old jukebox for his man cave. It had needed a little work and a buddy of Cruz's had pointed him toward a local restoration chain. The manager had claimed all the electrical components needed replacing. He called Ford from the back and introduced him as his best electrician. Ford had looked over the piece and Cruz had checked out Ford. He was big—like a sexy bear. Tall and cuddly. Solid. His dark blue gaze had landed on Cruz, and Cruz had been lost. To this day, Cruz couldn't recall what Ford said. He had lost his ability to hear with his heartbeat thumping loudly in his ears. Truthfully, Cruz had instantly wanted many people in his life. Ford had been different. It was like Cruz would die if he didn't have him. Ford hadn't made him beg or jump through hoops. He hadn't complained when Cruz worked too much or didn't see him for too many days in a row. Ford never bitched about anything period. Maybe that was why he had been so easy to take for granted.

Cruz hadn't known Ford wanted more. Now he realized he should have seen it. He should have given Ford everything without Ford having to beg for it. Now it was too late. It was funny how hindsight really was twenty-twenty. Cruz was a piece of shit. He had treated Ford like a booty call. Ford had told him that a thousand times in a thousand ways without actually saying the words. Cruz hadn't been listening. Now Cruz didn't know how to take it all back. He needed help.

Pure determination had Cruz brewing a pot of

coffee. He needed to get sober. His liquor-soaked brain couldn't rub two coherent thoughts together much less come up with a whole plan. When Cruz's mind cleared, he knew exactly what he needed to do. He had to talk to Jason. When Cruz hired Jason almost seven months ago, he hadn't expected to meet such a steady guy. Jason had met the love of his life on a Friday and had moved in with the guy by Monday. Cruz had thought the decision was nuts and would lead to nothing but disaster. The pair had proven him wrong. They were strong and accepting of each other in a way Cruz had never seen before. Jason would know what he should do.

With a plan set, Cruz got to work. He showered and went through the daily motions, killing time until his shop opened for the day. Cruz made sure he was good and sober before heading out. Unfortunately, Jason was nowhere to be seen. Cruz checked the paint booth where Jason usually spent his day doing custom paint and artwork. He wasn't there. Cruz headed for the break room. Only Eddie, his upholstery guy, was there grabbing a drink. Cruz stared at the vending machines, lost in thought. Had hitting Raiden driven Jason to quit? Cruz was under the impression they had worked things out. He had apologized several times. Maybe he needed to do more. After all, Cruz had practically accused Raiden of cheating when he spotted the guy at the casino with another man. There was no way Cruz could have known Raiden was working at the time and the other guy was a client. Of course, if Cruz wasn't such a hot head, he might have asked questions before flying straight into attack mode, forcing Raiden to put himself bodily in front of his client to spare him from Cruz.

"How's it going, boss?"

Eddie's question snapped Cruz from his inner musings. "Where's Jason hiding?"

Cruz wondered what it said about him that Eddie didn't look surprised Cruz had ignored his question. "He called in sick."

Fuck. That couldn't be a good sign. Jason hadn't quit, but not coming in suggested he might be weighing his options. There was nothing for it. Cruz would have to go by Jason's house. Ford planned to move in two months. Cruz didn't have time to fuck around. Without a word to Eddie, Cruz headed back out. His shop ran fine without him. He didn't necessarily have to be there unless there was a big financial decision to make. Right now, he had a more important deal to land. He could not lose Ford. It just couldn't happen.

THE HOUSE WAS MUCH NICER THAN DESCRIBED online. Of course, Ford had seen pictures, but he had also half expected to arrive in Phoenix and find he was being scammed. It was a real concern with the way people falsely posted other people's property for rent online, got the deposit, and then disappeared. That was why Ford had insisted on this tour before handing over a dime. The place seemed too good to be true. That was usually the first warning sign of a scam. But wow, the house was gorgeous. While it was on the small side for most people's tastes, Ford was only one person. He didn't need four bedrooms and three bathrooms. A two bedroom and two-bathroom house was the perfect size for him. In fact, it was still more space than he needed.

Ford flashed the guy giving him the tour a smile. His name was Bay. He was a doctor, and he smelled like he had money. In other words, he smelled delicious—just like Cruz. "This place is great."

Bay nodded. "It was my grandmother's house. She left it to me when she passed a few months back. I don't need it, but neither can I part with it."

"Lucky thing for me." Ford wished he wasn't awkward. He hated that he sounded like the guy's grandmother dying was a lucky break for Ford. Now Ford didn't know what to say.

To his relief, Bay moved the conversation away from the topic of his dumbassery. "What has you moving here from Vegas?"

Ford moved from room to room, eyeing every space like he hadn't already seen it. "My workplace is opening a new location here in a few months. They offered me the manager position at the new store. The place doesn't open until July, but I have to be here early so I can hire and train a new staff."

Bay clasped his hands behind his back and cocked his head to one side. He looked genuinely interested in everything Ford said. "What do you do?"

Ford forced himself to stop moving and focus his full attention on Bay. He hated the anxiety that made him uncomfortable with new people. "I'm an electrician. The company where I work does restoration."

"I have to admit, you're not what I expected," Bay said, taking Ford by surprise.

Ford knew exactly what Bay meant. He hadn't expected a Harley-riding tattooed miscreant when he agreed to let Ford look at his rental property. Ford couldn't help but fuck with him a little about it, because he knew a doctor did not want to rent his grandmother's house to someone like Ford. "What do you mean?"

Bay shifted from one foot to the other. He matched Ford in height. That made it a little harder for Bay to avert his gaze and hide his discomfort. They were eye to eye. "You just sounded different on the phone."

Ford's smile grew. For some reason he couldn't explain, Ford enjoyed making Bay uncomfortable. "How so?"

Bay's dark blue gaze latched on to Ford. His discomfort vanished. "To be honest, you look a little rowdier than I expected."

Even Bay's haughty honesty didn't steal Ford's smile. Being openly challenged by someone with money and success had Ford's blood pumping. Life had been empty and dull for a really long time. It didn't feel that way now. Ford looked down at his body and spread his arms wide. "I guess I probably do look that way. In truth, I'm pretty boring." Once the truth started pouring out, Ford couldn't stop. "I haven't been on a real date in years, and I've binge-watched the same TV series fifteen times in the past year. Normally, I'm in bed by ten and I've been at the same job for eighteen years. I guess my outside doesn't match my inside any longer, but I understand if my appearance scares you away from renting to me."

Bay's expression shifted, showing his confusion. He was a good-looking guy. Ford obviously had a thing for expensive and out-of-his-league men. "I'm not scared. If I gave you that impression, then I apologize." Bay smiled. It was breathtaking. "I have a terrible tendency toward honesty and was simply making conversation. You don't look anything like you sound on the phone. Truth be told, you're a pleasant surprise. You have no idea how tired I am of showing this place to college-aged kids who'll probably destroy the place within a month. I'd much rather rent the place out to a grown man."

A smile stretched Ford's lips. "Even a too-rowdy one?"

Bay's eyes flashed with laughter. "I thought you said you're boring."

A spark of something lit in Ford's chest as he stared at Bay. "Maybe there's some life left in me." Even Ford heard the flirting in his tone.

"Would you like to get lunch?"

Ford blinked at Bay's sudden offer. Bay's cheeks pinked. He looked ready to bolt. Ford's surprise disappeared. "I think I'd like that."

GUT-CHECKED

Bay smiled while still looking shy.

The spark in Ford's chest grew. Maybe Ford would survive without Cruz. It was possible his heart wasn't dead after all. There were other sexy brats in the world besides Cruz. Ford needed to get started on his new life. Bay looked like a great first step.

THE HOUSE WHERE JASON LIVED WITH HIS SEXY other half was less than ten minutes from work. It was a nice place in a great neighborhood and Cruz really looked at Jason's life for the first time since hiring him. He didn't think Jason needed him any more than Ford. Cruz liked choosing employees who were not only highly talented but also really needed the work. In fact, he purposely kept his ear to the ground, looking for people who were in the same boat he had been fifteen years ago. He paid them well and treated them good. That was how Cruz kept amazing employees loyal and gave them a second chance on life. Almost a year ago, one of Cruz's clients from Florida had told him about a guy who really knew his stuff. They had gone on to say Jason was not only highly skilled but in desperate need of a fresh start. Cruz had listened with his heart, since he too had escaped abuse through his business. After taking a look at a few pictures of Jason's work, Cruz knew he had to have him. He had offered Jason a great salary and snagged him. Jason hadn't let Cruz regret that decision. But now Cruz wondered if maybe he had patted himself on the back a little too much over helping Jason. Cruz wasn't sure Jason needed him at all. Just like Ford.

With that depressing thought in mind, Cruz rang the doorbell. He pushed the doorbell twice more and almost gave up before Jason answered. He looked confused by Cruz's presence.

"Hey. What's up?"

"You didn't come to work," Cruz answered like an idiot.

Jason blinked. "Raiden has the flu. I had to take him to the doctor. I have sick days," he added, as if Cruz was there to challenge him.

Cruz waved away Jason's words. "Of course. That's not an issue. I just need to talk to you."

While glancing around, Jason rubbed the back of his neck. "All right. Well, you can come in if you want, but like I said, Raiden has the flu. You might not want to risk it. The doctor gave me a prescription to cut back on the chances of me catching it, but you know... flu."

Yeah. Cruz couldn't risk that. He only had two months left with Ford. The last thing Cruz needed was to get sick. "Let's talk out here, if that's okay."

With a nod, Jason stepped outside and pulled the door closed behind him. His light green gaze focused on Cruz. "What's up?"

He was a gorgeous guy. Tall, blond, and muscular. Tattooed and every bottom's dream. But Jason knew all those things about himself and that wasn't the least bit appealing to Cruz. Cruz loved a clueless man. That was exactly why Cruz needed Jason's help.

"I did something really, really stupid."

Jason nodded. "We've established that, but if you've come to apologize again, I have to warn you that Raiden is in no mood to hear it."

For a split second, Cruz had no idea what Jason was talking about. When it dawned on him, he quickly wiped that away. "No. I mean, yeah, hitting Raiden was dumb too, but I'm talking about something else." Cruz took a breath, because—honestly—he had no idea where to start. Words burst from him without Cruz having to think about it. "I've been seeing someone for about three years now, and he's moving away in two months because he doesn't think we're a real couple."

Jason kept his thoughts hidden behind a closed expression, leaving Cruz feeling hopeless. "You've been with someone for three years, they're leaving you, and you're here talking to me."

It took all of Cruz's willpower not to dance in place with impatience. "Yes. Raiden and you are like a power couple. You're perfect together and I need help. I need advice or something."

"That was a nice thing to say about Raiden and me, but I need more to go on if you want advice. Why doesn't this guy think you're a couple if you've been together three years?"

Cruz bit his lip. He hated exposing himself like this. "It's possible that I never really established that we are a couple."

Jason visibly fought against showing any reaction. Cruz could practically see his mind churning. "What lines did you establish?"

Cruz deflated a little more by the second. "That we were sleeping together."

Jason's chest expanded as he took a deep breath. He pinched the spot between his eyes. "Okay. So you say you have two months, right?"

Cruz nodded. "That's when his new job starts in Phoenix."

"Then you have to be in his face every second

26

over the next two months." Jason nodded sharply as if his mind was set. "Don't let up, and I'm not talking about being in his bed. You've obviously already done that. It's time to give him all the pieces of you that you've denied him. Be there. Buy him gifts. Take him out on real dates. Surprise him with overwhelming gestures. Sweep him off his feet. You have to make it impossible for him to walk away from you."

Cruz didn't necessarily feel better, but Jason had motivated him. "I can do that," Cruz said, nodding. He knew he could invade Ford's life, but he wasn't sure Ford would accept any lavishing of gifts as genuine coming from Cruz. "What if this looks exactly like it is? A last-ditch effort to keep him here."

Jason shrugged. "Who cares? If you're genuinely set on keeping him, then it's time to act desperate."

"Okay." Cruz slapped Jason across the back. "Thank you. I'll let you get back to taking care of Raiden. I really appreciate the advice." Without a backward glance and with his mind locked on to his next move, Cruz jogged down the porch steps.

"Cruz."

Cruz froze and glanced over his shoulder. "Yeah?"

"Good luck."

With a wink, Cruz headed for his bike. He had at least one stop to make before heading to Ford's. He had some ideas on how to make Ford smile. Three years had given him some good memories of them to work with. His excitement to see Ford had him making quick time of everything. It wasn't until he turned onto Ford's street that it occurred to Cruz that Ford was probably at work. He breathed a sigh of relief when he spotted Ford's SUV parked in the driveway. That spurt of hope died away when his knock went unanswered. Cruz circled the house and looked for Ford's Harley. It was a nice day. If Ford didn't have to work, he had likely taken out the bike. It was gone. Cruz's eyes fell closed. He rubbed his chest. The desperation to get started begging was immense. He needed this fixed. Cruz didn't deal with long-term stress well. He pulled out his phone and found Ford's number.

Cruz: *You're not home.*

Ford: *No. I'm in Phoenix, checking out a few places for rent.*

Fuck. Cruz fought the urge to chuck his phone. Ford was already trying to settle in a new state. Cruz needed him here.

Cruz: *When are you coming back?*

Ford: *I'm driving back later tonight. Why?*

Cruz: *I was hoping to see you today.*

Ford: *Why aren't you at work?*

Cruz: *I want to see you.*

The three dancing dots that showed Ford was typing kept jumping on the screen. Cruz couldn't decide if Ford was writing a book or if he kept changing his mind about what he wanted to say. The dots disappeared. No message came. Five minutes passed before Cruz accepted that Ford didn't intend to respond. If he had, Cruz might have stood there all day. Ford's silence broke something inside Cruz. He had a feeling it was his fucks that were crushed, because he headed straight for the spare key hidden in a fake rock in Ford's flower bed. If Ford planned to drive back tonight, Cruz would wait. Ford would fucking talk to him and let Cruz beg him to stay. There was no other option to Cruz's mind.

The sight that met Cruz as he let himself inside had Cruz deflating. There were already boxes packed, marked, and stacked in every corner. This wasn't a decision recently made. Ford had known about this move for a minute. They talked every night and Ford hadn't said a word. Cruz dumped his gift for Ford on the couch and headed down the hall. Ford's bedroom wasn't filled with boxes like the living room and kitchen. Of course, Ford didn't hoard a lot stuff. In fact, he was a bit of a minimalist. He owned one bottle of cologne and exactly one bottle of every other toiletry. Ford's space wasn't crowded with things he didn't use. His bedroom was dark and clean. He had a bed, dresser, nightstand, and nothing else.

As usual, Ford's bed wasn't made. His dark blue comforter and sheets were balled up in a heap in the center of his bed. Cruz sat. His gaze skimmed the room. The walls were completely bare. Not even a single photograph marred the white surface. Cruz couldn't recall if they had always been that way or if Ford had already packed away everything. Cruz should know that. He had been in this bed dozens of times. Cruz couldn't remember ever looking at Ford's walls. That detail said a lot about Cruz. Mostly, it said Ford was right to leave.

Cruz found himself stretching out in the spot where Ford slept every night. Maybe he didn't remember the walls, but Cruz recalled every detail of the first night he spent in this bed. He could picture the way Ford looked at him as he stripped Cruz bare. There had been so much heat in Ford's eyes that Cruz expected to burst into flames, but Ford hadn't moved fast. He had savored Cruz—like he never expected Cruz to grace his bed again. Ford had been slow. Methodical. He had made Cruz beg. Cruz rolled to his side and buried his face in Ford's pillow. It smelled like him. With his eyes closed, Cruz breathed in Ford's scent. He already missed falling asleep on Ford's chest. Even Cruz didn't understand why he hadn't recognized how important those moments had been. Maybe he had believed he could call Ford anytime he wanted him. It was possible he had ignored Ford when his mind was locked on the next big job. Hindsight was an ugly thing. Cruz would make this right. He had to make this right.

LUNCH WITH BAY WENT FASTER THAN FORD expected. He truly thought he would be uncomfortable with Bay. They weren't the same in any way. While Ford enjoyed his job, it wasn't a calling, and he could move on to something else at any point. Being a doctor was different. That was knowing a path and sticking to it for life. Ford was thirty-eight, and he had never figured out what he wanted to be when he grew up. Sometimes, Ford felt like a mistake. It seemed he should be passionate about something in life, but the only obsession Ford had ever had was Cruz. Surely that made him broken in some fundamental way. Ford thought too much time with Bay would remind him of all those things. Instead, Ford found himself covering his mouth to stop laughing. Bay was fun and funny. He didn't give Ford time to think about anything else.

"Do you think I could convince you to stay tonight and have dinner with me too? I don't get many days off, but today happens to be one."

Ford shook his head. "I wish I could say yes, but I can't."

Bay didn't let up. "What if you didn't need a hotel room?"

A snort escaped Ford, but he couldn't stop smiling. "I have to work tomorrow."

"I realized a half second too late how that sounded," Bay said with a wince. "Honestly, I planned to offer to let you stay at the rental property until you needed to get back. I know you have to get back for work, but I hope I didn't scare you away."

"No." Even Ford heard the honesty in his answer. "I've had a great time today. You make me wish I could stay."

Bay blushed. He dropped his gaze to his feet and toed the ground. His shaggy hair fell over his eye and

Ford fought the urge to push it aside. They had been standing in the driveway of Bay's gorgeous house for over an hour while Ford tried to convince himself to leave. Bay kept telling stories about his childhood and Ford didn't try to make it stop.

When Bay met his stare again, the blush was gone. He visibly squared his shoulders. "Here's the thing. When you come back, I'll be your landlord and it'll probably be highly distasteful for me to ask you out again, but I want to. Do you think you would feel at a disadvantage if I asked to see you again?"

Because Ford recognized the honesty and integrity behind Bay's question, he chose to be every bit as open and truthful. "I don't know." The disappointment in Bay's expression had Ford rushing to explain. "For the past three years, I've let someone treat me unfairly. Moving here is a new start for me and I don't want to go back to feeling like I'm dating above myself, so I need to just tolerate whatever way I'm treated. I know what you're asking isn't the same, and I think you're pretty amazing, but I don't know if I would feel like I should take whatever you dish out. That doesn't mean I would say no if you asked."

A small smile hovered on Bay's lips. His gaze moved to a spot in the distance, as if he turned inside himself as he thought over Ford's confession. "I'm recently divorced," Bay said suddenly, surprising Ford. His gaze met Ford's again, and he looked steady in that moment—like a man people could depend upon. "He got bored with being the doctor's husband, and I found him in bed with someone else. I'm not very good at dating. Honestly, I liked being a husband. It was comfortable. Dating isn't comfortable for me. Like, if there's an emergency, I'm your guy. I'm great under the pressure of a health crisis. Otherwise, I'm awkward and strange. I don't know what to talk about with anyone, so I talk too much or not at all. You have no idea how many times I've chosen not to do things I want to do just because I thought I might have to sit and talk with people I don't know. So getting back out there and dating is like... a fucking nightmare." Ford felt those words to his soul, and he couldn't stop hanging on every word. Bay's smile turned kind. "When you get settled here, maybe we could be friends, and then—once you get to know me, and if you don't feel like I would make you less, then maybe you'd let me kiss you."

Ford took a step closer. Bay's lips parted in surprise as he correctly surmised Ford's intentions. Ford took advantage and claimed Bay's lips. Bay kissed nothing like Cruz. That was Ford's first thought, and it gutted Ford. While he had known he wouldn't get over Cruz in a couple of days and he probably wouldn't fall in love with the first person he touched, Ford didn't want to compare kisses. He couldn't stop. Cruz kissed slow and practiced—like a man with all day to please. Bay kissed hard and hungry—like he enjoyed getting fucked the same way. Ford forcibly slowed things down. He held Bay's jaw and kissed him the way he wanted. The way Cruz kissed Ford. Just the thought had Ford pulling away. Ford didn't want to give up, but neither did he want to hurt someone who had already been destroyed by a husband.

"Is it okay if I text you?" Ford truly wasn't ready to completely throw in the towel.

Bay nodded. "I'd like that."

Ford thought maybe he would too. Maybe he wasn't ready to date someone else, but Bay was nice. It was possible that nice was exactly what he needed. If only he could stop pining for Cruz. Maybe he could move on someday. Not today, but maybe one day.

THREE

THE ABILITY TO FEEL HIS ASS HAD DISAPPEARED at hour four of his ride home. It normally took a little less than five hours to travel between Vegas and Phoenix, but a wreck on the interstate had added another hour to his trip. Ford was tired and dirty. He wanted a shower and his bed. While he was also starving, food could wait. Every discomfort fled as Ford pulled into his driveway and spotted Cruz's bike. He shook his head as he climbed from his Harley as he realized Cruz was already inside. Cruz always took whatever he wanted without thought. It didn't surprise Ford at all that Cruz would break into his house.

The place was dark as Ford came through the door. Ford didn't know what he expected, but it wasn't the silence he found. After a cursory look around, he headed down the hall. Cruz was asleep in Ford's bed. A smile pulled at Ford's lips as he stared at the man in his spot. With one arm tossed over his eyes, Cruz slept like the dead. He was just so goddamn beautiful. Ford's throat swelled at the sight of him. He wished harder in that moment than he ever had that Cruz loved him, because Ford loved Cruz. It sat on his chest. Love choked the life from him all hours of the day because Cruz did not feel the same. But love was all Ford felt when he looked at Cruz, despite Cruz not feeling the same. Ford's love didn't care it was alone.

Ford turned away and slipped inside the bathroom. He quietly undressed and started the shower. While carefully keeping his mind blank, Ford felt the water until it turned hot before stepping inside. With his eyes closed, Ford let the water rain down on him. Behind his eyelids, Cruz waited. The image of him stretched out and sleeping peacefully in Ford's bed was etched on Ford's brain. Damn, he was just messy blond hair and perfect lips. Cruz was supermodel beautiful. Ford didn't think he could be blamed for his weakness. The crazy thing was, while Cruz was perfection on the outside, it was his kindness toward others that really swept Ford off his feet. Cruz genuinely cared about people. He felt his employees were his family, and he worried about their wellbeing. Cruz talked at length about solving homelessness and wondered aloud about he could help curb the suicide rate. He felt things deeper than anyone Ford had ever met, and he left Ford feeling awed. Ford didn't think he could be blamed for getting his heart stolen. He just wished it didn't hurt so much.

While Ford washed his hair, he tried changing the image in his mind to Bay. Cruz was too large. He took up too much space. Ford couldn't push him aside. In fact, Ford could still recall every detail of the day they had met. Brian, Ford's boss, had called his name, asking him to come take a look at a jukebox for a customer. Ford had cleared the doorway between the back of the store and the front. Goddamn. He swore angels sang. Ford had immediately been one hundred percent certain Cruz was straight. Then Brian had left them alone. Cruz had dropped his gaze to Ford's feet before slowly meeting his stare again. Heat had nearly flayed Ford's skin from his body. Before Ford could recover, Cruz said, "Tell your boss I have another machine at my place I want you to take a look at it." And Ford knew all the way to the bottom of his soul that was the exact moment he had gone wrong with Cruz. He said yes. If Ford had shut Cruz down in that moment, maybe Cruz would have chased him. Respected him. Ford was a goddamn idiot. Always had been.

The shower curtain ripped open. A nude and sexy Cruz stood on the other side. Without a word and before Ford could recover a brain cell, Cruz stepped inside. His body collided with Ford's. Ford reacted out of instinct. He dipped his head and touched his lips to Cruz's. Just like the day they met, Ford knew he made a mistake there was no coming back from. Knowing didn't stop him. They were already nude. Cruz's erection already rested against Ford's bare skin. There were some things Ford couldn't refuse—like carrot cake, free hockey tickets, and Cruz. This was the kiss. The one he loved. The kiss no one else gave.

"I don't want to fuck you in the shower." Ford changed angles and sucked Cruz's bottom lip. "I want to take you to bed and treat you the way you deserve."

A stuttered breath escaped Cruz. "I don't deserve anything."

That was so untrue, and that was the problem. Cruz should have someone waiting for him when he came home each night. That person should warm his bed and make sure he ate. Cruz would enjoy a liquid feast for every meal without anyone taking care of him. He needed someone and Cruz would never find his soulmate as long as Ford stayed in the way. Ford's throat burned. He dropped his forehead to Cruz's shoulder and squeezed his eyes shut. Cruz was the one for Ford and Cruz didn't feel the same. No one understood how much that pain crushed his throat every hour of the day.

Cruz stroked Ford's back. "You're right. Let's go to bed."

Ford turned away and killed the water. Before he turned back, Cruz began drying Ford's skin. As always, there was no mad rush to the bed. Every second was a savored moment. Ford couldn't look away as Cruz thoroughly wiped him down. The sight of Cruz's tattooed hands on Ford's body was intoxicating. Ford knew he still had time to shut this down, but maybe he needed one last night with Cruz. He would treat each moment as the last, because it was. Ford could brand this night on his brain to warm him when he never met anyone else. After kissing Bay, Ford had spent that six-hour ride home with nothing but his thoughts, and he came to terms with a few things. The biggest truth he owned was that he probably wouldn't get his happy ending. Ford likely wouldn't fall in love and get married. He doubted there would ever be anyone who looked at him like Ford looked at Cruz. Ford was okay. He would live the rest of his life quietly without the constant longing for what he couldn't have. One last night with Cruz made sense.

"You're incredibly beautiful." Ford blinked at the sudden compliment. Cruz kept his gaze locked on his hands as he spoke. "I think I should've been telling you that. I guess I assumed you knew." Cruz's gaze lifted. He met Ford's stare. "I guess I assumed you knew a lot of things."

Ford took Cruz's hand and headed for bed. He didn't want to talk. At the edge of the bed, he sat and pulled Cruz to stand between his knees. Ford automatically brushed his thumbs back and forth across Cruz's hips. It was entirely possible that Cruz had a million tiny flaws. Ford couldn't see them. All he saw was this guy who made him want more of everything. More kisses. Longing looks. Time. Ford pressed his lips to Cruz's chest. Cruz straddled Ford's body and pushed, forcing him onto his back. Ford knew he could take control, but it felt too good beneath Cruz. He stole his chance to stroke every place he could reach. Cruz rocked as his mouth covered Ford's. All thought fled Ford. Considering Ford always overthought everything, Cruz was pretty damn powerful if he wiped Ford's mind clean. Cruz bit Ford's bottom lip. Ford swore his entire body vibrated.

"Did you see your present? I left you a surprise on the couch."

Ford tugged Cruz's hair, forcing his head back and exposing his neck. "I was too busy looking for you," Ford confessed as he sank his teeth into Cruz's neck. Ford was hit with a sudden and powerful need. He didn't want to be soft and slow. Ford wanted Cruz to remember him. It was necessary to Ford's soul that Cruz look back on this night and still feel Ford. In one quick flip, he had Cruz pinned beneath him. He caught a flash of Cruz's surprise before Ford claimed his mouth. He dug around one-handed in the cubby of his old headboard until he found the tube of lube and condoms he kept there. Ford wasn't gentle as he fingered Cruz, oiling his asshole while getting him hot. As he ripped open the condom with his teeth, Cruz bit his chest. Something inside Ford's brain snapped. He was tired of showing Cruz love. Maybe Cruz deserved his hate.

Ford changed positions and forced Cruz onto his stomach. He bit Cruz's back and ass as he impatiently rolled the condom down his length. Once he finally had it in place, Ford didn't play with Cruz. He fucked him. With all the anger and hurt Ford had kept hidden, he shoved his way inside and thrust. Cruz white-knuckled the headboard, holding himself in place while Ford sawed in and out of Cruz hard and fast. The sound of skin slapping against skin and gasped breaths lingered in the air. Ford bit and sucked every place he could reach, leaving his mark. He pulled Cruz's hair and tore at his skin. Cruz's body sucked him, tightening and releasing Ford's cock over and over again, making Ford insane. He was angry and turned on past lunacy. He wanted to take everything from the hot hole he owned in that moment. Then Cruz cried out, his body convulsed, and Ford's mind cleared. Even in his rage, he had somehow pleased Cruz. Ford hadn't taken anything back in this encounter. In fact, as Cruz's body massaged an orgasm from Ford, Ford lost more than his cum. Another piece of his soul chipped away. Ford wasn't sure he had enough left to give to anyone else. Cruz had already stolen all of him.

FOUR

FROM HIS SPOT ON THE BED, CRUZ WATCHED Ford quietly move around the room, getting ready for work. He hadn't turned on the lights and demanded Cruz leave. In fact, it was obvious he tried his best to not wake Cruz. Cruz decided to take it as a win. Things had been... different between them last night. Cruz couldn't explain it. In the past, Ford had always moved slow, taken care. Made Cruz feel loved, if he was being honest. Last night had felt more like rage. It had still been hot, and Cruz had definitely ruined Ford's sheets, but Cruz wasn't so sure where he stood any longer. Maybe he really was too late. When Ford approached the bed, Cruz quickly closed his eyes and pretended to sleep.

Ford stroked his hair. "Hey, sexy. I have to go to work."

Cruz groaned. He didn't want Ford to leave.

A sexy chuckle rumbled from Ford. "I know. You don't have to get up." His lips skimmed Cruz's. "Go back to sleep. I just wanted to let you know I'm leaving."

"Have a good day."

With one final sweet kiss, Ford headed out. Cruz gave him an hour head start before going after him.

Meek's Restoration was a small place with maybe ten employees. Most of those worked outside the physical location, driving from job site to job site, working on various projects. Ford and the owner Brian were usually the only two inside. Brian flashed Cruz a welcoming smile as Cruz came through the door.

"Cruz. Wow. That's a face I haven't seen in ages." Brian circled the counter and shook Cruz's hand. "What brings you by?"

Cruz took a good look around, as if checking out the few restoration pieces they had for sale before focusing on Brian again. "I've got a big project for you."

The way Brian's eyebrows rose and his eyes lit, Cruz knew he would get his way. Brian was a middle-aged workaholic who loved making money. Cruz was the same and knew how to play that card. Brian immediately bit. "Tell me all about how I can help."

Cruz dove in. "I bought ten of those old arcade games. The big ones from back in the arcade days. I'm adding on to my game room for when my nephews visit." This was all complete bullshit and Cruz couldn't stop. "All the games are from the eighties and nineties and need various levels of work. I wasn't in a huge rush to get them all done at once, but then I heard a rumor that Ford is leaving you."

Brian nodded along. His dark brown eyes practically had money signs flashing in them. He scratched at his salt and pepper beard. "He's not exactly leaving me. Just the state. I'm opening a new location in Phoenix and Ford is taking over management there."

Cruz shook his head. He let his disappointment show. "I really hoped to get Ford to do the work. You know I don't trust anyone else."

Brian smiled. "That's no problem. He's still got time before the new place opens. I'm sure he could get everything working and looking like new before his move if he dedicates all his time to it and the price is right."

"Is that going to be a problem for you? I mean, if I could go ahead and steal him and hang on to him until the move, that would be great."

With a careless wave, Brian brushed off Cruz's question. "I've already hired his replacement, so I won't be shorthanded. Let's get some terms ironed out and he's yours for the duration."

"Perfect." Even Cruz heard the triumph in his voice.

"Let me go grab the paperwork and I'll send Ford your way."

Cruz nodded. "Sounds great."

Brian disappeared into the back of the shop. A moment later, Ford stepped out. His blank expression gave nothing away. Cruz tried not to let that get under his skin.

"I hear you own me for the next two months."

Damn. Even Ford's tone didn't give away his feelings on that matter. "Almost." Cruz winked. "I still have to pay."

Ford's chest expanded on a deep breath. For a moment, he simply stared at Cruz, looking slightly defeated. When he spoke, he sounded confused. "What are you doing, Cruz? First, you break into my house, and now this. I don't get it."

Cruz could have lied. He didn't want to do

that. In fact, he needed Ford to see exactly how serious he was about this. "I'm doing what I should've been doing all along. I'm putting you first."

Ford looked like he barely suppressed an eye roll. "You know this doesn't change anything, right? I've already accepted the position in Phoenix. My deposit is paid on a house there. I'm moving away. It's too late to change that."

Cruz gave Ford a sharp nod he didn't mean. "This changes nothing. Got it. Do you need to grab your stuff before we go? I still need to sign some paperwork with Brian."

Ford rubbed the spot between his eyes. "I guess I'd better grab my tools."

"Great idea. Otherwise, Brian might get suspicious."

A low and sexy-sounding growl escaped Ford as he walked away. Cruz couldn't stop smiling. He had Ford exactly where he wanted him. Even knowing that, he didn't feel confident until he had Ford shuffled out the door. "Follow me to my place. I'll drop off my bike and then we can get going."

"Where are we going?" Ford didn't sound unwilling. That was a start.

"It's a surprise." Cruz was making things up as

he went. "Speaking of which, did you ever look at the gift I left you?"

Ford shook his head. "Sorry. I left a little late this morning and forgot to check it out."

Cruz waved it off. "It'll be an added bonus when we drop by your place so you can pack a bag later."

Damned if Ford didn't look like he might burst a blood vessel. "Why am I packing a bag?"

"It's a surprise," Cruz and Ford said at the same time, except Ford sounded sarcastic as opposed to Cruz's playful tone. This was fun. Cruz should have been showering Ford with annoyance every day before now. He had never realized how sexy Ford's indignation could be.

Ford shook his head and started toward his SUV. Cruz straddled his bike and watched Ford's every step. Goddamn, he had a gorgeous ass. It was big and round. Perfect. Cruz swore his stomach growled. He would bite that ass for the rest of his life, even if he had to kidnap Ford to do it. In fact, maybe that was exactly what he would do. He wasn't above anything at this point.

FORD TRIED REALLY HARD NOT TO THINK ON THE

drive to Cruz's house. Cruz was up to something, but Ford couldn't figure out his end game. Ford felt certain he had made himself crystal clear that his plan to move was set in stone. For some reason all his own, Cruz kept pretending like Ford leaving wasn't happening. None of his current predicament made sense. Yes, Cruz was his best friend, and yes, they spoke every single day, but Cruz had never given any indication that he couldn't survive without Ford. Cruz's reaction to this move was... odd. Cruz knew everyone. He wouldn't get lonely. The guy was sexy as fuck. His bed definitely wouldn't get cold. Ford wasn't this important, so why? Why was Cruz doing this? Ford shook his head. Cruz confused him.

At Cruz's place, Ford parked at the edge of the driveway, leaving room for Cruz to get in and out of his garage. As Cruz passed him and pulled his Harley into the garage, Ford ate up the sight of him. Damn. Cruz never stopped making all the muscles in Ford's body tense with desire and anticipation. Being seen with someone like Cruz—someone who turned every head—it made Ford feel special. He knew everyone envied him when they saw them together. Ford's momentary happiness slipped. Cruz was like a beautiful illusion. The sight of him made people smile until the truth sank in that they were still alone.

Ford slid from the vehicle, determined to keep his heart free from Cruz's game.

Cruz stood inside the open garage door waiting for him. He wolf-whistled as Ford approached. "Damn. You are a sexy one. What's your name, big fella?"

Ford shook his head at Cruz's antics. He barely managed to fight his growing smile. "What's the plan for the day?"

Cruz felt of his pocket—like his phone buzzed. He pulled out the device and checked the face. A line appeared between his eyebrows and he quickly put his phone away. "Let's get some lunch before you pack your bags."

Ford didn't budge. He knew Cruz's every expression as well as he knew his own. "What's wrong?"

With a shake of his head, Cruz motioned toward his F-350. "Nothing. Get in the truck. It's eating time."

For a moment, Ford wondered if anyone had ever hurt themselves suppressing eye rolls. "For fuck's sake. Quit pretending to be someone you're not. I know that look. You're worrying about something work related. So what's going on?"

Cruz pulled a face. "I'm not pretending to be someone I'm not. I'm trying to be the guy you want and not the workaholic I am, but if you're going to be pissy about it, Jason called out again today. I'm not sure a major project we've been working on will get done on time without him."

Ford spent a minute processing. He didn't know whether to complain first or help. He decided to hit it all at once. "I never said I wanted you to stop working. I love that you're passionate about what you do. Let's drop by your shop before lunch and get shit lined up to get done on time."

It was Cruz's turn to refuse to budge. Irritation flashed in his eyes. "You're moving because I wouldn't change, so don't say you don't want that."

So Cruz was choosing to fight. Cool. Ford had some arguing in him. "I never said you work too much. In fact, I'm pretty sure I never said a goddamn word about your job. I said I wanted to fucking matter to someone. Your job doesn't have a damn thing to do with you always waiting until two in the morning, after you've exhausted all other options, to call me and ask me to drive across town to fuck you. The fact that you're a workaholic doesn't make you not love me. Don't fucking put the blame on me if you can't grasp that someone might need to be special and not a last resort." Ford walked away. He was headed back toward his SUV without a single thought. Ford hated being angry. He didn't like to argue. While it was possible he had kept things bottled up too long, he still didn't want to have this discussion. They were already done. End of story. Anger and yelling changed nothing. Cruz buying him for the next two months didn't mean shit to Ford.

"How do you feel about sanding steel and using primer?"

Ford stopped in his tracks at the question. His eyes fell closed. He didn't turn. "I've done it a time or three."

"I think if we get all the prep work done, Jason should have plenty of time to work his magic when he gets back."

Ford nodded and changed direction, walking with his head down toward Cruz's truck. He didn't know why he kept doing this horrible thing to himself, throwing himself against a brick wall for Cruz. If he walked away right now, Ford doubted Cruz would stop him or get him fired. There was nothing keeping him glued to Cruz, except Ford's inability to deny Cruz the tiniest thing. It was only a matter of time before this turned into a real problem. In two months, Ford had to leave. He couldn't let Cruz stop him. It was one thing to constantly compromise his pride. It was a whole other to end up unemployed and homeless.

They were halfway to Cruz's shop before either of them spoke. Cruz was the first to break. "For the record, you are important to me, and you've never been my last option. I just truly am a workaholic. If I'm not at the shop, I'm usually networking at the biker bars or trying to talk casino owners into hiring me to design their next big giveaway. I have five guys who depend on me for their livelihoods. If I stop hustling, they lose out. You don't like going to bars, so I didn't want to bug you with that. I never meant for you to get lost in the mix, but I guess the squeaky wheel gets the grease, and you never complained. It wasn't until you dropped the bomb that you're leaving that I realized I had already failed you."

The defeat in Cruz's tone had Ford staring hard at his profile. With his elbow on the door and using his fist to prop up his chin, Cruz stared at the road. His expression matched his tone. A light switch flipped in Ford's head. Cruz understood he had already lost Ford. Ford still didn't get why Cruz wanted to spend every second with Ford now that it was too late to save them, but Cruz wasn't toying with him. Ford's decision to leave hurt Cruz. That had never been Ford's intention.

Ford leaned Cruz's way and set his hand palm up on the console between them. Cruz shifted positions and linked fingers with Ford. Ford brought their joined hands to his mouth and kissed the back of Cruz's hand. "I'll still be just one phone call away," Ford said, breaking the promise he had made to himself when he had decided to move. He had told himself he would sever all ties with Cruz. Ford couldn't do it. "Phoenix isn't really that far away." Ford wanted to bite off his tongue. He couldn't stop trying to make Cruz happy, no matter the personal cost. "I won't make the drive at two a.m., but you can visit." Goddamn. Why couldn't he stop?

"We'll cross that bridge when we get there, I guess." He looked Ford's way and flashed him a bright smile. "I'm glad you're here now, though."

Oddly, Ford was too. No matter the current circumstances, Ford loved Cruz. Always would. Any amount of time at all with him was better than a second spent anywhere else. Ford made a decision. He would take what he could get. No matter how much it hurt when it came time to leave, he would accept this time with Cruz. He made a conscious choice to see it as a blessing rather than a curse. Maybe the next two months wouldn't change anything, but Ford wouldn't fight anymore. He didn't possess the strength any longer. Worse than that, he no longer had the desire.

HAVING FORD WITH HIM AT WORK ALL DAY FELT amazing. Each time Cruz looked over and saw Ford working at his side, he smiled like an idiot. By the time they were finished for the day, Cruz was more than ready to have Ford alone again. Every chance he got, Cruz caressed Ford's sexy ass on the sly. Ford never once complained. Cruz couldn't stop. He kept finding reasons to squeeze behind Ford while he worked. The more Ford didn't protest, the bolder Cruz became.

Cruz molded against Ford's back and reached around him. "Let me just get this." Cruz wasn't quick about it. As he leaned past Ford, grabbing an empty coffee cup in an excuse to touch Ford, Ford turned his head and lightly kissed Cruz's ear. Cruz froze. His eyes fell closed. It was the smallest of gestures, but Ford had initiated the contact. Eddie strolled into Jason's booth where they worked, leaving Cruz no choice but to step away. With his heart in his throat, Cruz tossed the empty coffee cup in the trash. He didn't meet anyone's gaze as he tried to look busy while Eddie inspected their prep work for Jason.

Eddie released a low whistle. "Damn, Dude. You do good work."

"Thanks. Cruz told me what to do, and I did it. I'm sure you could've done better."

Eddie snorted. "I'm an upholstery guy. If it's leather, I can do anything you want, but everything else is beyond me. You should work here full time. We got an opening."

Before Ford could respond, Cruz cut in. "I'm going to go call Jason and see if he'll be in tomorrow. I'll be right back."

Ford flashed him a smile. Their gazes met and held for just a second. Cruz swore something was different between them since that argument in Cruz's truck. Cruz forced his eyes away and strolled from the room but didn't go far. He stopped the moment he was out of sight, eavesdropping. As he had suspected, Ford was obviously waiting for Cruz to be gone before responding to Eddie's suggestion.

"I'm sure working here is great, but I just

accepted a management position in Phoenix, so I'll be living there soon."

"Oh, no." Eddie dragged out the words, sounding genuinely yet obnoxiously crushed by Ford's news. "That's going to kill Cruz. You're like his best friend and stuff. Are you two doing the long-distance thing or calling it quits after the move?"

A pregnant pause stretched on, choking Cruz with anticipation. When Ford finally responded, he sounded confused. "What do you mean?"

Eddie being Eddie, he had no couth. "Like you two have been dating a long time. Are you giving up? Obviously, with the shop and all, Cruz can't go with you. You breaking my boy's heart or what?"

Cruz was torn between the need to save Ford and the desire to hear his answer. Instead, Cruz chose a different path. He walked away and headed for the break room, deciding he didn't want to know after all. It was too soon. He needed more time to convince Ford to stay. If he heard Ford say nothing would make him stay with Cruz, Cruz might do anything. He was stupid like that. Instead, Cruz dug out his phone and pulled up Jason's number. With his phone on speaker, he set it on the counter and listened to it ring while he fixed a cup of coffee. Jason answered on the fourth ring.

"Hello?"

Cruz couldn't help but smile at the sound of Jason's voice. He genuinely liked Jason. "How's Raiden today?"

"Still sleeping a lot. His fever seems to be breaking, though. I'll be back tomorrow. That Fat Boy is due out soon. I can't miss another day and get it done on time."

"The prep work is done."

"Thanks for that," Jason said, sounding relieved.

Cruz nodded like Jason could see him. He sipped his coffee before responding. "It's no problem. I had help."

"How's Operation Convince-Ford-to-Stay going?"

A snort escaped Cruz. "Not well, so far. I think he's pretty dead set on leaving me."

"I'm sorry." Jason sounded genuine. "It would kill me to lose Raiden. I wouldn't wish that on anyone, so I'm really rooting for you. When Raiden and I were in Florida for my brother's wedding, I had this huge revelation about the intensity of love and how much it factors in to the mental stability of the world. Nothing is more important than being with the person who keeps you sane. Everything else is just busy work for the idle mind."

That was profound and true. Cruz loved this shop. It was important to him, but he also realized it was his creative outlet and financial support system. This place wasn't his rock, tying him to life. Ford had always been what he looked forward to the most. Everything that happened all day every day were only stories he saved to share with Ford. Insanity was all he had to look forward to if Ford left. He realized Jason was probably expecting a response.

"Agreed, so I'll keep working on things on my end, and you work on making Raiden better. Maybe we'll both hang on to a slice of sanity."

"Will do, boss. I'll see you tomorrow."

"Yep. See ya," Cruz said, tapping the face of his phone and hanging up.

"It sounds like Jason will have the bike out on schedule."

Cruz's gaze snapped toward the doorway. Ford stood there waiting. Cruz had no idea how much of that Ford had heard. He decided to brazen things out. "Yeah. Raiden is still sick, but his fever is coming down."

Ford looked thoughtful as he nodded. "Jason sounds soulful. Are you ever going to tell me why you hit Raiden?"

Cruz saw a lifeline and pounced. "I'm dumb and

have a hot temper. You know me. I never stop and think before making the worst possible impulsive decisions. I was at Lombardi High-Roller Casino, trying to convince the manager to hook me up with the owner so I could talk to him about designing a bike for a casino grand prize. While we were talking, I spotted Raiden there with another guy."

Ford sucked a hiss through his teeth. "Not good."

Cruz nodded. "I saw red. The guy was looking at Raiden like Raiden was on the menu, and I snapped. Before I knew what was what, I was across the room and swinging. Raiden jumped in front of the guy." Cruz shrugged and sipped his coffee, leaving Ford hanging for the sake of suspense.

"So he was with another man and protecting him, but you were in the wrong? What the fuck?"

A chuckle slipped from Cruz. He loved Ford. No matter what, Ford was always on his side. "Actually, it turns out that the guy he was with is the owner of Lombardi High-Roller Casino. He's Raiden's longtime friend, Jason knew they were together, Raiden was working at the time, and I'm an asshole."

For a moment, Ford stayed silent. Cruz could practically see his mind working, turning everything over in his head. "You're a good friend." Cruz snorted, but Ford waved it away. "No, seriously. Things might not have ended ideally, but you saw a guy with your friend's man and believed he was a threat. You stepped up. That's what friends do."

"Maybe," Cruz said, shoving his phone in his back pocket. "That doesn't change that I ended up hitting Raiden and I could've lost a valuable employee and friend over it. I'm also banned from the casino."

A smile exploded across Ford's face. "You've never been one to half-ass things."

Except being with Ford. Cruz had half-assed that. Now it was time to remedy that. "You helped me out of a tight spot today. Tell me how I can repay you."

Ford's eyes swam with laughter. "Maybe you could put me out of my misery with this whole surprise thing."

"Maybe I could cook you dinner instead," Cruz shot back. "Are you still a sucker for manicotti? We could pick up the stuff on the way to your place. I cook and clean while you kick back."

"My place?"

Cruz nodded. "No rushing out in the middle of the night to see me."

"My car is at your place."

A smile that felt evil even to Cruz pulled at his lips. "No running away from me. Plus, with your car at my place, no one can claim you weren't working when we disappear."

Ford's eyebrows rose. "Disappear?"

Cruz tossed his coffee cup in the trash. "You'll see."

Ford huffed. It was an adorable sound. Cruz couldn't stop smiling. He hadn't had this much fun in years. Tormenting Ford was a blast. Cruz couldn't wait to see Ford's face tomorrow. After all, Cruz was whole-assing this thing with Ford now. Ford was about to get swept off his feet. Fun times were ahead. He would see.

No matter how Ford pled, Cruz wouldn't give him any hints about this big surprise. Truthfully, Ford wasn't as curious as he pretended. He liked the way Cruz's eyes lit with excitement at the topic. Cruz was like a kid with a secret. Ford imagined Cruz's secret would involve him throwing his money around. Ford had never cared about Cruz's money or what Cruz could buy him. All Ford wanted was more of this. The way Cruz had been acting all day.

That was something money couldn't buy and exactly the version of Cruz he couldn't resist.

Cruz carried the bags from the grocery store while Ford unlocked the door. He swore he could feel Cruz's intense stare boring into the back of his head as they stepped inside. Ford tried to shake the feeling he was being stalked. As Ford stepped through the door, his gaze automatically slid toward the couch, where Cruz claimed he left a gift for Ford. A fluffy white teddy bear sat waiting. Ford didn't know how he missed the guy when he had left for work that morning. His only excuse was he had been running late and not paying attention.

Ford headed straight for the gift. "Well, now. Who are you?"

Cruz chuckled. "Don't you recognize him?"

Ford looked over his shoulder with his eyebrows raised. "Should I?"

A snort followed Cruz into the kitchen.

Ford sat and eyed the bear. He honestly didn't recognize him. Cruz reappeared. He shook his head as he crossed the room. When he reached Ford, he dropped to his knees between Ford's and took the bear away before sitting on the floor between Ford's feet.

Cruz held the bear out and inspected him. "We

should search online what the most expensive teddy bear is, because I bet this guy fits the bill."

Ford quickly sat forward and grabbed the bear. "No way. Is this the same one?" He turned the bear from side to side. "Oh my god. You spent like two hundred dollars trying to win me this bear at that restaurant with the game room. How did you finally get it?"

"They're selling their prizes now. You can either win so many tickets or pay the equivalent in dollars."

With his eyes locked on the bear, Ford shook his head. "I can't believe you remembered that. That was like our second date. Back when I still believed we were going somewhere other than bed." Ford laughed as he made the confession. His gaze slid Cruz's way.

Something dark passed over Cruz's features and he pushed to his feet. "I'll get dinner started."

A groan reverberated off the walls of Ford's mind. He hadn't guarded his words. It hadn't been his intention to be an ass. The bear truly was a thoughtful gift. Ford may as well have thrown it in the trash. He tossed the bear aside and went after Cruz. At the kitchen counter, Ford molded against Cruz's back. He wrapped his arms around Cruz and kissed the side of his neck. "That was a really sweet thing to do. Thank you. You blow me away."

He felt Cruz shrug. "I guess I should've realized it would only remind you how much I've failed at this."

Ford dropped his forehead to Cruz's shoulder.

Cruz stepped sideways out of his hold. "Go sit down. I've got everything under control in here."

"Are you kicking me out of my own kitchen?"

"Yep," Cruz said, flashing him a smile. It looked fake as hell.

Ford practically leapt, overcoming him. "Nope. This is where all my favorite foods are." Ford claimed Cruz's mouth. The second he felt the tension drain from Cruz, Ford loosened the button on Cruz's jeans.

Cruz chuckled against his lips. "I'm trying to make you dinner."

"I'm trying to eat," Ford said, slipping to his knees. He peeled open the front of Cruz's jeans, going straight for the dick he wanted. Cruz's semi-hard cock stiffened in Ford's mouth. Ford immediately lost himself to the act. With his eyes closed, he sucked and licked while clinging to Cruz. He no longer cared about anything beyond the dick in his mouth. Ford loved the texture scraping against his tongue. He toyed with Cruz's crown, circling it and lapping up every salty drop of pre-cum. Cruz tugged at his hair and moaned. Ford was numb and deaf to it all. His entire focus was on his task. Ford's cock ached in his jeans, as if the pleasure was his. When cum filled his mouth, Ford swallowed, savoring every drop. He still didn't stop sucking. Ford wasn't finished yet. He loved the way Cruz squirmed too much to let him go. Maybe he would make Cruz beg before the end. It wasn't too far-fetched of a dream.

FIVE

AFTER ANOTHER MORNING OF BEGGING, CRUZ still wouldn't tell Ford where they were going. When they reached the airport, Ford felt like his suspicions were confirmed. Cruz was throwing his money around as a surprise, surprising no one. Ford was a tad bit confused when he saw their destination, though. Knoxville, Tennessee. That didn't sound like any place Cruz would want to go.

"Why Knoxville?"

"You'll see." Cruz's singsong answer was the most Ford could get out of Cruz. After landing in Tennessee, Cruz picked up a rental SUV, and they were off. The longer they drove and the more signs they passed, the more Ford's suspicions rose. Cruz stopped just inside Pigeon Forge at a packed

Walmart. He bought a disposable ice chest, ice, beer, and snacks. Their next stop was a management office, where Cruz picked up a set of keys. With every passing mile, Cruz's mischievous smile grew and Ford's thoughts on where they were headed solidified by the second.

When Cruz led Ford inside a small cabin, the past washed over Ford. It had been twenty-plus years, but Ford remembered every detail. "Dear god." Ford stared at Cruz in awe. "How did you know about this place?"

Cruz grabbed the ice chest full of beer and headed for the back deck. The deck overlooked a stream where Ford had caught his first fish. It was the same view as Ford remembered. "This is the same cabin as the one you shared with your dad, right?"

Ford didn't answer right away. He filled the seat next to Cruz as Cruz settled down. Shock rocked him to his soul. "Yes, but how did you know that?"

Cruz looked his way. With his eyebrows drawn together, he seemed genuinely confused by Ford's question. "I know everything about you because I listen to everything you say. Like, I know your dad brought you here for a guys' weekend of fishing when you were sixteen. The two of you had such a great time, hanging out and talking, he said you two would come back every year. He died six months later, and you never got to come back." Cruz kicked his feet up on the porch railing and stared at the streaming water as he spoke. Ford couldn't look at anything other than him. "I know you hate broccoli, but it was the only vegetable your mom seemed to cook. You were best friends with your cousin Doug growing up. He was two years older than you and stuck up for you any time someone tried to bully you about being gay. I know he killed himself at seventeen and now no one in your family talks about him, like he's some sort of black mark on the family, but you miss him every day." Ford's eyes burned with unshed tears, but Cruz didn't stop. "You visit your mom at least twice a week. You're a huge dog lover, but you don't want a dog because you worry you won't be able to afford its care. Maybe other people don't know you, but I do." Cruz turned up his beer while Ford was left speechless.

They had spoken on the phone every night for so long that Ford hadn't realized how much of himself he had shared with Cruz. He certainly hadn't realized Cruz had been paying attention. Ford wanted to give the same speech, listing everything he knew about Cruz. Ford couldn't make his tongue work as a huge revelation washed over him. He couldn't claim to know Cruz the same. Ford usually did all the talking. If Cruz talked about anything, it was work or work related. Why hadn't Ford asked questions? Another thought sneaked in and stole his ability to speak. Maybe Ford was the one who had been using Cruz for sex. Perhaps he was the one who hadn't tried for more. After all, Cruz knew him, but Ford didn't know Cruz. Fuck. He was a bastard.

Ford refused to believe it was too late. "It occurs to me that you never talk about your parents."

Cruz's beautiful blue eyes slid Ford's way for a second before he focused on the water again. "I guess there's nothing to tell, really. We see each other on holidays. For the most part, they don't make much of an effort to speak to me outside those designated dates. I don't reach out to them either."

Now that Ford realized he didn't know everything about Cruz, he wanted to learn every detail. "Why?"

A small smile touched Cruz's lips and slipped away just a quickly. "The road and phone lines run both ways and eventually you get tired of being the only one traveling them. While they have nothing against me being gay, they mourn the loss of who they wanted me to be too much to spend a lot of time with me. My mom was a stay-at-home mom, and she wanted to be a stay-at-home grandmother. My dad worked really hard to support us so she could be those things. I disappointed them."

Ford was flabbergasted. "You're so successful. I'm having the hardest time picturing your parents being disappointed in you. How old were you when they learned you're gay?"

A sexy chuckle fell from Cruz's lips. "When I moved in with my boyfriend at twenty."

The urge to flap his arms like a lunatic nearly had Ford levitating in his seat. He couldn't believe his ears. Ford hadn't known Cruz lived with anyone. "You used to have a live-in boyfriend. For how long?"

Cruz finally focused on Ford. A line appeared between his eyebrows. "Ten years. Have I not told you this story?"

"No," Ford said, dragging out the word. Ten years. Cruz had lived with someone for ten fucking years and Ford hadn't known.

Cruz's expression cleared. He looked away. "Oh."

Ford thought he would burst a blood vessel at Cruz's flippant response. Cruz dug another beer from the ice chest and went back to staring at the stream. Before Ford could melt down, Cruz completely wiped his mind.

"He was abusive."

Ford's entire body deflated. Cruz did not look like the kind of guy who got abused. He was muscular and somewhat intimidating. Cruz was beautiful and nice. Ford couldn't imagine anyone hurting him.

Cruz looked down at his body. "I didn't always look like this. At twenty, I was scrawny and kind of shy. By the time I left Shawn, I was a different person—hot-tempered and distrustful. I had always sort of escaped into art and creating beautiful things in an ugly world. Even though I worked as a mechanic back then and presented a normal face to the world, I was a wreck. It was embarrassing to be in the position I was in. So, eventually, I left. I started working out. Stopped dating. In fact, I stopped doing much of anything that didn't benefit me. I didn't see men as beneficial to my life, so I didn't bother with one." Cruz nervously picked at the label on his beer. "Obviously, I realize I didn't walk away unscathed. I'm a hot-tempered bastard now who works too much." His gaze slid Ford's way. "I ignore people for things. The last fifteen years have been busy but quiet." A gorgeous smile stretched Cruz's lips. "Except for you, of course."

Once again, Cruz stunned Ford into silence. Cruz's claim implied Ford was the only person in Cruz's life since leaving his ex. That seemed unlikely, but Cruz was a workaholic who had been focused pretty intently on building an extremely lucrative business. It was just that, if Cruz was being completely honest with Ford right now, then Ford moving away from this man was the dumbest fucking decision of Ford's life. Goddamn.

CRUZ COULDN'T BELIEVE HE HADN'T TOLD FORD any of this. They spoke so often and much that Cruz hadn't realized this topic hadn't been broached. Then again, Cruz was pretty careful to stay away from anything past fifteen years ago when he had gone all in with Iconic Stylin' Rides. Apparently, there hadn't been any late-night drunken confessions with Ford. That was odd. Cruz really thought they'd had this conversation.

In better news, Ford seemed genuinely blown away by Cruz's surprise. That was good. Cruz couldn't recall the last trip he had taken. He really wanted this to be a memorable vacation. If Ford chose Phoenix, then Cruz wouldn't likely take any time off again anytime soon. In fact, this might be the last break Cruz had.

"I see why your dad and you wanted to come back to this place. It's gorgeous here. Peaceful."

Ford didn't respond.

Cruz glanced his way. The intensity in Ford's expression stunned Cruz. "What's wrong?"

"I'm trying to avoid asking where this guy lives and if it's too late to go kill him."

A laugh burst from Cruz. "Yeah. You're a little late. Not only am I no longer a helpless kid who needs protecting, he died in a car accident like five years after we split. It was a road rage incident from what I understand."

Ford shook his head. A small smile hovered on his lips, spiking Cruz's curiosity again.

"What?"

Ford snorted out a laugh at the question. "It seems so funny to me now that you were like, 'we should go fuck' the very first time we met when you're so uninterested in anyone else."

Cruz's cheeks hurt from smiling. "Yeah. I guess I was a bit wowed by you and acted very out of character in response. But then again, I wasn't missing my chance. It was like, there he is, the one for me." Cruz chuckled. His smile slipped away as reality settled in. It was possible he should have tried a little harder to work on himself after leaving Shawn. Cruz hadn't planned to ever fall in love again. For that reason, he hadn't bothered trying to fix the damage Shawn caused in Cruz's ability to have a healthy relationship. He supposed none of that mattered now. The more time he spent with Ford, the more Cruz realized maybe Ford was better off without him. Cruz would likely go right back to working too much. Ford deserved a good man. A normal guy. He polished off another beer. Maybe, if nothing else, Ford would look back on these last couple of months with Cruz and smile. Cruz could turn himself into a good memory.

"I wonder if they still have that amazing steakhouse here?" Ford asked, changing the subject.

Cruz glanced around, as if truly looking for the place even though they were in the middle of nowhere. "I don't know. A wildfire swept through here a few years back. Truthfully, when I set out to book this trip, I half expected this cabin would be gone. We can drive around later and look for it, if you want."

"You're drinking," Ford reminded him.

Cruz eyed his bottle and then set it aside. If he stopped now, he would be good to drive in a few hours. "We got some time."

"Maybe we should check out the hot tub in the meantime."

The hot tub on the other end of the deck was out of the sight of prying eyes. In fact, the entire cabin was pitched as being private and secluded. They could do anything anywhere and no one would see. Cruz stood and took off his shirt. He headed for the jacuzzi without looking back. He peeled back the top and started the jets before unbuttoning his jeans. His gaze slid Ford's way. Ford was already on him before Cruz could gauge his thoughts. He held Cruz's face and kissed him deep. It wasn't sexual. In fact, their kiss felt deeper than that.

Ford pulled away but held on to Cruz's face. He kissed Cruz's nose before pressing his lips to Cruz's forehead. "Thank you for this. I recognize how much thought you put into this surprise."

A lump formed in Cruz's throat. He pulled out of Ford's hold and finished stripping. "Maybe you'll look back on me and smile," Cruz said once he found his voice. Still, he couldn't look Ford's way as he climbed into the hot tub. Cruz already felt the truth all the way to his soul. Ford wouldn't choose him over a normal life in Phoenix. When it came to matters of the heart, people never chose Cruz. This would be no different.

MAYBE YOU'LL LOOK BACK ON ME AND SMILE. Those words haunted Ford throughout the rest of the night. They found the steakhouse. It had moved locations but was still in business. After dinner, they walked around town and checked out some tourist hot spots. Cruz bought him some crazy novelty souvenir made from a corncob and an expensive 3-D puzzle based on one of his favorite books. Each time Cruz proved how much he knew about Ford, the more Ford thought his move was a mistake. By the time they made it back to the cabin, Ford was ready to scratch away at his brain. He no longer knew the truth about them. In fact, Ford was more confused than he had ever been in his life. What Ford knew for sure, though, was that he loved Cruz. That didn't seem to have any chance of changing.

"Do you want a beer?" Cruz asked over his shoulder, heading toward the fridge.

Ford looked up from where he had been digging

through his suitcase to focus on Cruz. "No, thank you. I'd rather have you."

Cruz turned and cocked his head as he focused on Ford. "You already have me."

A smile that felt evil even to Ford pulled at his lips. He grabbed a condom from his bag. "That's not exactly what I meant. Go drink your beer. When you're ready, come to bed." Ford put the condom between his teeth and held it there, freeing his hands to grab the rest of his bedtime things. He flashed Cruz a smile with the condom between his lips before walking away. He knew Cruz would follow shortly behind.

Cruz didn't make him wait long. As Ford tossed lube and the condom onto the bed and stripped off his shirt, Cruz molded against his back. His hands worked on the button of Ford's jeans as he bit Ford's shoulder.

"I can sit around drinking beer anytime I want, but I'd always much rather be sitting on your dick."

Ford dove for the condom. "Sitting it is, then." He shoved down his jeans and hurriedly suited up. "My lap is the perfect seat." He sat on the edge of the bed, dick out and waiting. "Strip," Ford demanded as he lubed his waiting cock.

Wickedness flashed in Cruz's eyes as he peeled

away his clothes. His huge, hard dick sprang free of his jeans and Ford's eyes latched on to it. His mouth watered. Cruz stroked himself. "Is this what you want?"

Ford nodded, but his gaze never wavered from the erection that called his name. "Come sit on Papa's lap and I'll make you feel good." Nude, Cruz moved to stand between Ford's knees. Ford kneaded his ass before turning him around. "Right here, sexy." He held his dick in place and urged Cruz's hips back and down until his cock was pressed against Cruz's hole. Cruz sat, impaling himself. A loud pant escaped Ford. His fingers automatically sought Cruz's erection. He stroked.

"Goddamn," Cruz breathed, sounding turned on.

Ford wrapped one arm around Cruz's chest to keep him from falling on the floor and went to work. He played with Cruz's balls and jacked his cock. Cruz whimpered and squirmed on Ford's lap, making Ford's eyes roll back in his head. "That's it, baby. I know what you like."

Cruz tried lifting up and fucking himself on Ford's erection. Ford refused to let him move. "Just feel me." He stroked—slow and steady. Cruz's asshole tightened as Cruz tensed. Ford lightened his touch, teasing. "Let me tell you a story."

Cruz whimpered.

There was no mercy in Ford's heart. "Once upon a time, I was working away and minding my business, when the most beautiful man I've ever seen pushed his way into my life. He took me home and stuck his fingers in my ass. No one had ever touched me like that before."

"Oh, god."

An evil smile pulled at Ford's lips at Cruz's desperation. "He made me shameless. I begged for those fingers. Then he licked my asshole and blew my mind. He pled for me to stick my dick in his ass and make him fly. I was a blushing mess. No one so beautiful had ever wanted me before. I wasn't used to the dirty talk and foreplay. So I moved slow." Ford tightened his grip on Cruz's dick and slowly stroked. "I didn't want to hurt the sexy angel. His asshole looked so tight and unused. My dick looked huge when it stretched him open. He made sounds I'd never heard before. I was scared as hell that I was hurting him. Then, as I pushed all the way to the hilt inside him, his entire body convulsed. Hot cum hit me on the chin. I didn't even get to thrust. His tight body sucked my dick so quick and hard that I came. I swear to God I lost sight in my left eye. But his asshole kept sucking. I kept gasping. I knew right then I never wanted to be inside anyone else ever again." Cruz's body jerked. Cum shot across the floor. Ford kissed his neck and gasped for air as Cruz's asshole massaged him, suckling him. Ford's mind glitched. He spoke without thought. "That was the moment I fell in love with you." A cry tore from Ford's throat as an orgasm ripped through him. Being with Cruz had always been this way. Cruz rocked him. He didn't need to bounce on Ford's dick and fuck him hard. All Cruz had to do was let Ford inside. Ford's mind did the rest. He knew he had his cock inside the sexiest man on earth. That was goddamn mind-blowing in itself. Cruz shouldn't let Ford soil him, but he did. He shouldn't want Ford, but he did. Ford was nowhere near good enough, but he would be. From the moment Cruz had shown his heart inside this cabin, Ford had known the truth: he couldn't leave Cruz behind. That meant he needed to think. Things weren't so cut and dried any longer. Ford needed to figure out his life, and fast, before he lost the greatest man he had ever met. He couldn't lose Cruz.

CRUZ COULDN'T STOP STROKING FORD'S stomach. With his ear pressed to Ford's chest, Cruz savored the sound of Ford's heartbeat caressing his eardrums. The sensation of Ford's stomach rising and falling with each breath fascinated Cruz. He truly loved everything about Ford. Always had. Why had he always been so scared to say as much? After all, Ford had said the words. It wasn't like Cruz was alone in his feelings. Was he that fucked up? Cruz didn't think he honestly believed Ford would use the confession to crush him the way Shawn had. Plus, Shawn had been a lifetime ago. Surely Cruz wasn't still a head case because of him. Cruz had a suspicion things were a little closer to home when it came to Ford, like how Ford hadn't—not even once— hinted at wanting a real relationship before dropping the bomb about leaving.

"I have a comment and then I have a question." The words were out there before Cruz could stop them.

Ford tilted his chin down, trying to meet Cruz's eye. "All right."

Cruz did his best to avoid eye contact. "You're my best friend."

"Same. So, what's your question?"

"Why didn't you just talk to me?" Cruz didn't

mean for his inquiry to come out sounding quite so angry, but there it was. Still, he tried to keep going and tone it down. "I mean, we talk damn near every single night. Why didn't you just tell me that you felt neglected or whatever? I'd like to think I wouldn't have let you down."

"Because I'm dumb." Ford's response surprised Cruz enough that he lifted his chin and met Ford's stare. A sad smile briefly touched Ford's lips. "It's not that I thought you're a mind reader or anything. I just hoped you would choose me over everything else without me asking you to do so. Isn't that how it works?"

Cruz shrugged without thought. "I don't know. I've never been in a healthy relationship. If there are rules, I don't know them. I really kind of need you to use your words."

"Fair enough."

A smile exploded across Cruz's face and he couldn't really explain why. Ford was just so damn amenable. Cruz's smile slipped away. He supposed he should follow his own advice. "I guess I should do the same. So," he scratched his nose, dragging out the moment, because he was chicken shit. "The truth is that I love you and I really want you to stay, but I know I can't ask that. Phoenix is a great opportunity for you. I get why you want to go." The more he talked, the more he realized he should just shut the fuck up. "I don't know. I was just saying all my thoughts and not really going anywhere with this. Now I'm depressed, but I hope you find what you're looking for, even though I know it's not me. I won't bring it up again." Cruz pressed his lips together to make himself stop talking.

Ford rolled, tucking Cruz beneath him. He settled down between Cruz's thighs and cuddled up. It was like Cruz was cocooned in a blanket of sexy man. Ford caressed Cruz's chest. "Do you remember that time you had the flu, and I took off work for a week to stay with you so I could take care of you?"

"Yes." Cruz had no idea where Ford was going with this.

"Then I got the flu and had to miss another week of work, but you wouldn't see me until I was better."

Damn. "Yeah. I had that big bike rally I couldn't miss. That's one of the biggest events that keeps us in business."

"I know," Ford said, sounding calm. "I'm not saying I don't understand. You have a lot of people counting on you. I'm saying that's just one example where taking your own advice and using your words would've made a huge difference to me. That was one more time when I felt pretty fucking insignificant to you. I hear what you're saying now. I see that you're trying. But I'm not so sure I can give up this huge of an opportunity to go back to being last in your life. I just need to think, okay?"

Cruz got it. He had already lost. "Okay." It tasted like a lie on his tongue. Cruz knew he had done a lot of shitty and neglectful things over the past three years. As much as he would like to think he had also done some good too, Ford had obviously been stewing over the bad for a while. Defeat settled into Cruz's chest. Maybe he needed to concede. It was possible that letting Ford go was the right thing to do. They would finish this trip and then Cruz would gracefully bow out so Ford could move away guilt free. He knew he would never go back to his old ways now that he realized what he had done. Unfortunately, there was no way he could make Ford know it too. He could already feel his heart breaking. Cruz automatically held Ford tighter. He wouldn't fall in love again. This part of life had been nothing but cruel to him. Cruz didn't have the strength to do it again. He wasn't sure he had any strength left at all.

SIX

Since Cruz was like a hyper child, incapable of staying indoors and doing nothing, they spent a lot of time walking around town. They drove between Pigeon Forge and downtown Gatlinburg, hitting all the tourist sites. Ford wasn't the least bit surprised when Cruz dipped inside a tattoo shop. He couldn't stop his laughter, though.

"Do you even have any blank skin left?"

Cruz flashed him a smile. "Some."

A guy with a huge beer gut and unkempt dark beard met them at the door. "You looking for some new ink?"

Ford wandered off and left Cruz to make a deal. Cruz was a talker. He could sell anyone anything and get shit for free like no one Ford had ever met. A smile touched Ford's lips. He was fucking amazing. Ford glanced over his shoulder. Cruz had his shirt pulled up, pointing at a small bare spot on his torso. With a snort, Ford went back to flipping through the posters on the wall. He had a couple of pieces here and there, but tattoos weren't cheap. Ford had too many other expenses to invest in useless things. Plus, he wasn't a perfect canvas like Cruz. Ford wasn't really toned, and he definitely wasn't hairless.

"He's squeezing me in now, if that's cool with you," Cruz said, pulling Ford's attention their way.

The tattoo artist jumped in before Ford could argue. "It'll only take me like ten minutes tops."

"Go for it. I'm good." Ford was good at keeping himself entertained. He was usually alone. Years ago, he had learned—if he hoped to do anything fun at all —he would have to do it by himself. He ate at restaurants alone and went to the movies. Truthfully, he was more accustomed to doing everything as a party of one. Ford didn't need anyone to entertain him.

Cruz reappeared before Ford had time to miss him. He was shirtless. A girl working behind the counter damn near fell off her barstool while leaning over to get a better look. Ford hid a smile. He got it. At forty-five, Cruz was better than most men half his age. Any lines he had gained from age only made him look sexier. It wasn't fair, truth be told.

"Come let your buddy know what you think."

Ford did as the artist bade, moving to Cruz's side. He inspected the new tattoo on Cruz's ribs. It was Ford's name. Ford's throat swelled.

"I tried to get him to get the emblem along with it, but he wasn't interested. We don't get a lot of Ford fans around here," the guy said with a laugh. "It's mostly Chevy fans in these parts."

Cruz looked ready to burst into hysterical laughter at the guy's blatantly wrong assumption. "I'm definitely partial to Ford."

Ford couldn't stop looking at his name permanently etched on Cruz's skin. With so many other images on Cruz's skin, it was possible no one would notice Ford's name. Ford knew it was there, though.

"Did you find anything you want done?"

Ford's mind wouldn't budge from what Cruz had done.

"Hey, Ford. Yo, did you find anything?"

Ford blinked, coming back to himself. He finally managed to focus on Cruz's face. "Did you say something?"

Cruz's eyes swam with laughter. He shook his

head. "If you want to get something, I'll pay for it."

The tattoo artist looked between them. His expression screamed shock. He didn't say anything, but it was obvious he had finally caught on.

Ford's shoulders squared. He focused on the guy who had written Ford's name on Cruz. "Do you have time for that?"

He nodded, seeming to snap out of his surprise. "Yeah, sure. If it's nothing big, I've got about half an hour before my next appointment."

Ford's mouth lifted in one corner in a sardonic smile. He couldn't believe he was about to do this. "I need a four-letter name on my shoulder."

"Oh, yeah. I definitely have time for that."

"Let's do it," Ford said. His gaze moved Cruz's way and stayed. Goddamn this man. He really did have Ford ten shades of fucked up. There didn't seem to be any end in sight. Nor did Ford think he wanted it to end. Ford was in a lot of trouble. Fuck his life.

WHILE CRUZ WASN'T ONE TO STAY INSIDE AND do nothing, Cruz wanted to touch Ford. Cruz still couldn't believe Ford had gotten his name tattooed on his shoulder. It was covered with Saniderm to protect it, but Cruz could still see his name staring out at him. He watched Ford grill shirtless and his eyes never wavered from the sight of his name. It was one thing for Cruz to get Ford's name on his skin. His body was covered in tattoos. Ford didn't have much ink. Anything on him would stand out. For Cruz, new ink meant nothing. It meant everything when Ford did it. Now Cruz couldn't stop questioning if that meant he planned to stay. Goddamn it. Ford was really fucking with him.

Ford turned and caught him staring. "You okay?"

"Of course." He forced a wicked smile to his lips. "I'm watching a sexy cooking show. I'm perfect."

With a shake of his head, Ford went back to preparing their meal. Cruz went back to staring at his name. A snort escaped him without thought.

"I think we fucked that tattoo guy up. He really thought I was a Ford enthusiast. Obviously, I am, but not the way he thought."

Ford tossed a quick look over his shoulder. His eyes swam with laughter. "Yeah. I don't think this town is used to people quite so open. At least he didn't refuse the job, I guess."

"Nah. It only took him a few minutes to do mine, but he chatted the whole time. I could tell he wasn't the type to care. Still, he did look a bit shocked when the truth finally sank in."

"I guess this really isn't our scene," Ford said as he shut the lid on the grill. He moved Cruz's way. "It's gorgeous here and I love it, but we couldn't freely live here."

The idea of living full time with Ford slammed into Cruz's chest, stealing his breath. He wanted that. He wished like hell things were different. Cruz couldn't believe how thoroughly he had lost someone who owned him.

"Stop."

Cruz blinked at the order. "Stop what?"

Ford went down on his haunches in front of Cruz's lawn chair. "Quit thinking about me moving away. I thought you'd agreed to let me think about things."

A laugh he didn't feel slipped from Cruz. "So you're allowed to think, but I'm not."

"That's right. Don't make me fight you."

Cruz's smile turned real. "You want to fight me now, is that it?"

"Yep." Ford sprang to his feet and playfully boxed around Cruz. "You're pretty solid, but I think I could take you down. All I have to do is this." Ford swept in and covered Cruz's mouth with his. He didn't hold back. His tongue fought Cruz's, licking and seeking more. Cruz found himself clinging to Ford's face, refusing to let him get away. Ford was right. This was all it took to make him go down. Cruz didn't plan to stop. Not ever. Ford was his.

"Our food is going to burn."

"Fuck that food," Ford said, sounding breathless as he urged Cruz from his chair. "I want to touch you. Let me touch you."

Fuck. Cruz didn't know how to resist Ford. No one had ever made him feel so wanted in his life. People had a lot to say, bullshit compliments and whatnot, but Cruz really felt Ford's desire. There was nothing fake about him.

Cruz found himself on his knees and tearing open the front of Ford's jeans. He was desperate to taste Ford. Ford tugged at Cruz's hair as Ford's cock filled Cruz's mouth. Cruz's desperation didn't ease. He needed Ford to understand there was no one else out there for Cruz. Ford could leave. He could run away. Maybe Ford could even start a new life with someone new. Cruz couldn't do any of those things. He had gotten Ford's name etched on his skin because it was already seared into his soul. Cruz knew he spread himself too thin and Ford lost out in that mix, but goddamn it. Cruz loved Ford. He needed Ford to feel it. Ford would feel it if it was the last thing he ever did.

THERE WAS NOTHING BETTER THAN HAVING Cruz on his knees, except for having Cruz on his cock, where Ford could taste his lips. With the hot, perfect suction on his dick, Ford had a hard time pulling away. His heart had him pulling Cruz back to his feet and rushing him inside. They stumbled several times, trying to keep kissing while making it back to the bed. Ford didn't bother closing the door. Nothing mattered as much as getting Cruz in bed. Ford kissed a path down Cruz's body while peeling off his jeans. He paused near Cruz's new tattoo. Ford didn't touch it because he knew it was sore. His eyes flipped upward. He met Cruz's stare. Cruz looked turned on and ready to get fucked.

Ford nodded toward the fresh ink. "When that heals, I'm tracing every letter with my tongue." As the promise fell from his lips, Ford realized he had already stopped making plans to leave. He was rearranging his future to include Cruz. Cruz rolled a condom down Ford's cock when Ford froze beneath the weight of the truth. He wasn't moving. Cruz was his future. He always had been. Tomorrow, they would go back to Vegas and Ford needed to accept reality. He couldn't live without Cruz. Ford slowed down. He was in love. Ford needed Cruz to feel it. He held Cruz's jaw, forcing Cruz to hold his stare as he pushed his way inside. The pressure in his chest was more than the need for release. It was his soul, trying to get closer to the other half of him.

"I love you." Ford was tired of not saying the words.

Cruz sucked in a gasp, as if Ford's love rocked him. "I love you too."

Ford pressed his forehead to Cruz's chest and thrust. His entire body electrified, leaving him exposed like a raw nerve. "Tell me you're mine," Ford begged against Cruz's chest.

"I'm yours."

Ford sucked in Cruz's scent, memorizing everything about the moment. Even if they went home tomorrow and Cruz went back to barely seeing him, Ford had this now. For the rest of his life, he would know Cruz had said he loved him and called himself Ford's. No matter what else happened in his life, he had been loved by Cruz. That was more than most people ever got. For Ford, it was a dream come true.

SEVEN

With Ford in the shower, washing away the airport germs, Cruz paced Ford's bedroom floor. He had told himself he would let Ford go once they were home. Cruz had sworn he would stop tearing the man in two and let him move on guilt free. Now that the moment was upon him, Cruz didn't know if he could do it. In fact, he had been back and forth on the matter a million times over the past week. Ford had gotten Cruz's name tattooed on his shoulder. Surely that meant something. All the waffling from never letting Ford go to letting the man move on was killing Cruz. He had chest pains and was pretty sure his hair was falling out.

Cruz stopped in front of the mirror above the dresser and stared at his reflection. Almost every inch of bare skin, excluding his face, was covered in ink. While he had always been a huge art lover, and his tattoos were an extension of that, his reasoning for each piece was more mental. He hated what he saw in the mirror. No amount of hitting the gym or covering his skin drowned the voices in his head. So he worked himself to death and just kept getting more ink. He was a mess inside. Always had been. For whatever reason, Ford had still fallen in love with him. Cruz wasn't sure he could give that up.

Ford's phone lit, catching Cruz's eye. He dropped his gaze without thought.

Bay: *I know it's short notice, but I'm in town for a conference. May I take you to dinner?*

For a moment, Cruz couldn't even blink. He hadn't meant to read Ford's message. It was just kind of there, staring him in the face. Another message popped up on the screen before Cruz could look away.

Bay: *I'm staying at Lombardi High-Roller Casino's hotel. I get a break at six. Let me know if you can join me in the hotel restaurant.*

Who in the hell was Bay? That wasn't a name Cruz had heard before. Where was he in town from? The only place Ford had gone in a long time besides his trip with Cruz was Phoenix. Did Ford already have someone in Phoenix? Before Cruz could storm the bathroom and demand answers, the phone vibrated on the dresser once more.

Bay: *I hope that kiss didn't scare you away.*

Cruz's knees gave out. He sat hard on the bed. He had no idea how long he stared at nothing before Ford reappeared. With a towel wrapped around his waist and water glimmering on his skin, he looked delectable. Cruz couldn't tear his eyes away. He always fell in love with people who destroyed him.

"I should go."

Ford nodded. He looked disappointed. Cruz wondered how much of everything was a lie. "I imagine you have a ton of shit to do after being gone a week." He picked up his phone, scrolled, and then typed a quick reply before setting it aside again. "I have a few things to do too." Cruz dropped his chin and looked at his chest. He half expected to find a knife in his heart. Ford closed the distance between them. He toppled Cruz onto his back. It wasn't hard. All Cruz's strength had fled at reading that message. Ford straddled Cruz's body. "You should call me when you get home tonight. Better yet, you should come back when you're done. I've gotten spoiled by holding you every night."

Damn. Ford was either the most beautiful liar

Cruz had ever seen or he had turned down that dinner date. Cruz didn't know how to feel. He had to know the truth, but his tongue refused to work. Ford kissed him, taking away the sting of betrayal. Cruz's shoulders relaxed. He would find out the truth for himself. Ford didn't taste like a liar. He was gorgeous. Of course, other men would want him. That didn't mean Cruz would accept him being with someone else. Bay, whoever he was, hadn't said Ford kissed him. He had said he hoped that kiss didn't scare him away. That sounded a little like an unexpected kiss. Maybe even an unwelcome one. Things weren't set in stone. Cruz would see for himself if he had been played. Then he would decide what do next.

LOMBARDI HIGH-ROLLER CASINO HAD A SMALL hotel attached that somehow managed to snag nearly endless conferences. Ford assumed the place had some labyrinth of ballrooms in between the hotel and casino that made the place the perfect spot for businesses hoping for a fun tax write off. The fact that Bay had asked Ford to meet him at this particular casino was the only reason Ford had agreed. Since Cruz had been banned from here, Ford felt relatively safe having a quick drink with Bay. It wasn't that he thought there was anything wrong with meeting Bay per se. They were only friends, or renter and landlord, except they had also kissed, and Cruz would likely punch first and ask questions last if he saw them together. Cruz wasn't exactly known for his calm temperament.

While sitting across from Bay, Ford realized it hadn't simply been heartbreak driving him to make a move on the guy in Phoenix. Bay was genuinely very hot.

"I'm glad you could meet me on such short notice. It's too bad you can't stay for dinner, though."

Ford probably could stay for dinner. With Cruz being out of town for a full week, he likely had a million things to do, leaving Ford to busy himself for the rest of the night. Ford didn't care. He had done something tonight too, and he needed to see Cruz as soon as possible before he lost his nerve. Dinner with Bay didn't fit with his schedule and wasn't where Ford wanted to be.

Ford rubbed the back of his neck. He needed to get this out of the way. "Can I be honest with you about something?"

Bay flashed him a laughing smile. "Well, yeah. I think most people prefer honesty."

"I don't think I want to move anymore," Ford said before he could change his mind. He really needed to hear himself saying the words out loud. Once the words were out there, they didn't sound as firm as they felt in his heart. "Rather, I know I don't plan to move."

Bay pursed his lips and slowly nodded. "Ah. I guess that explains why I haven't heard from you."

Ford pulled a pained face. "Yeah. Sorry about that. When I came to Phoenix, my mind was set. Then... it wasn't. There's something here I can't leave behind. Someone."

"This is an interesting turn of events."

Ford's head whipped around as Cruz's voice washed over him. "Cruz." Even to his ears, Ford's voice came out sounding breathless. Shock stole the wind from his lungs.

Cruz looked angrier and more hurt than Ford had ever seen. He didn't give Ford time to explain. "Here I've been spending every second trying to convince you to stay after you dropped the bomb about leaving and you're here with this guy." He motioned Bay's way without looking away from Ford. Cruz shook his head. Ford swore he could hear

Cruz's heart breaking, and he didn't know how to make it stop. Cruz didn't give him time to think. "You fucking gut-checked me by threatening to leave me, Ford. Well, I guess you got the reaction you were looking for. I've been sick thinking about you moving away from me, and you're already seeing someone else. But I'm the asshole, right? I'm the one always neglecting you.'

"Um, we're not seeing each other," Bay said, trying to cut in. No one listened. "We're just friends."

"It's not like that, Cruz."

Cruz swiped their drinks from the table and walked away. Ford flinched at the sound of shattering glass.

"Holy shit." Bay sounded thoroughly stunned by the show of temper. No doubt he was unused to people being quite so over the top.

A man in an expensive suit appeared at the edge of their table. Ford had never seen the guy before. "Sorry for the disturbance. May we replace your drinks? That man was supposed to be banned. I'm not sure how he got in, but I'll be having a word with security." He had a thick Italian accent and gorgeous blue eyes. Ford didn't give a fuck about any of that.

He focused on Bay. "I'm sorry. I have to go after him."

Bay waved him away. "Go. Just keep me posted."

"It is just the two of us now," the sexy Italian said as Ford walked away. "Would you like that drink?"

Ford didn't stick around to hear Bay's answer. Cruz had a head start and mind full of untrue thoughts. Ford had to get to him before he got away. Cruz could be damnably self-destructive when he wasn't in a good headspace. He spotted Cruz in the parking lot. Ford jogged to catch up with him.

"Cruz. Hold up. Would you just listen to me?"

Cruz spun on him so fast, Ford almost jumped back in fear of Cruz swinging. Instead, it was only the pain swimming in his eyes that punched Ford. "What? You have your way. I'm out of the picture and you can start your new life. It's too bad your plan to make me out to be the bad guy didn't work out, but whatever, right? You're already dating someone else, so what do you care?"

Ford bit back a growl. "I'm not dating anyone else. Bay is my landlord in Phoenix. He's just in town for—"

"Stop," Cruz barked, cutting him off. "I saw his text about you two kissing. I was standing at the dresser when it came in, and I saw it. So just stop.

Jesus, I can't breathe." Cruz rubbed his chest and looked everywhere but at Ford.

Ford took a breath. He had to fix this. "To be fair, I thought we were over when I kissed Bay, but that's where I stopped."

Cruz bent around the waist and braced his hands on his knees. "Dear god. It's even worse than I thought. You kissed him. Seriously, I can't breathe." He really sounded like he couldn't. Every word Cruz said came out on a wheeze. He sat on the ground.

Ford rushed to his side and dropped to his knees. He forced Cruz's chin up. Cruz's face was pale; even his lips seemed to have lost some color. "Holy shit, Cruz. Hold on." He dug out his phone and called 911. Ford didn't wait to ask Cruz if he needed help. He already knew Cruz would refuse.

"Fuck," Cruz growled before losing consciousness and dropping to the ground.

"911. What's your emergency?"

Ford spoke, but he had no clue what he said. He raced between trying to get help and trying to convince Cruz to wake. His breathing was shallow, and his heart raced. The way that Cruz had been rubbing his chest jumped to the surface of Ford's mind. He couldn't lose Cruz. Not now. Not ever. He had to wake up. Ford couldn't go on without him.

MANY TIMES IN CRUZ'S LIFE, HE HAD WOKEN UP in unfamiliar places, unsure of how he had gotten there, heavy drinking usually being the culprit. He had never woken up in the hospital. Cruz blinked at his surroundings. Ford sat quietly at his side.

"Why are you here? Shouldn't you be with your man?" Even to his ears, Cruz's voice sounded like he had been chewing on gravel.

Ford jumped to his feet to hover over Cruz. "Damn. You went down fighting and woke up the same." Even though laughter tinted Ford's words, worry swam in his eyes. "For the record, I'm with my man right now. How are you feeling?"

"Like my heart has been crushed."

A line appeared between Ford's brows. "Mentally or physically?"

Cruz thought it over. "Both."

Ford nodded. "They ran a bunch of tests, which you were kind of in and out for. Do you remember any of that?"

Cruz shook his head. "What's wrong with me?"

"They're checking everything just to be safe. It's possible you suffered a mild heart attack, but we won't know for sure until all the tests come back."

"Well, that's..." Cruz didn't know how to finish that sentence. Several descriptions sprang to mind: horrifying, par for the course, and just his damn luck were all top contenders. He decided to tackle the reason he had landed here instead. "Why did you make me think I could save us if I never stood a chance?"

Ford rubbed his arm, as if he needed to touch Cruz. "You need to stay calm."

A machine started beeping. "No. I just caught you having drinks with someone else. The time to be calm has passed."

Ford seemed damnably steady in the face of Cruz's rage. He kept rubbing Cruz's arm and trying to soothe him. "Stop. Just listen for a moment. If you stay calm, I will explain everything. Okay?"

Cruz nodded, because he didn't have a choice. He needed to know the truth.

Ford gave him a sharp nod, seemingly satisfied. "Bay is my landlord in Phoenix. Yes, I kissed him once. I thought you and I were over, and I knew immediately it was a mistake. He came to town for a conference and I agreed to meet him so I could give him back his keys and let him know I'm not moving."

Cruz blinked. "You're not moving?"

Ford shook his head. "I can't leave you."

The door opened and Ford turned away to focus on the woman who joined them. In blue scrubs with a white lab coat, she looked like a kid playing dress-up. She was a tiny woman with a head full of short blond curls. Her gaze moved between them. Ford retreated to his chair.

The woman focused on Cruz. "Hi there, Mr. Dalamar. How are you feeling? I'm Dr. Shannon."

Cruz forced himself to focus on his current circumstances. "Well, I'm here, so..."

"True," she said with a bright smile. "Can you tell me what happened?"

He tried to make his brain work. The last thing he recalled was shouting at Ford. He didn't want to say that.

Ford came to his rescue when he didn't respond. "He said he couldn't breathe and then sort of passed out."

Dr. Shannon looked between them, nodding. She unwound her stethoscope from her neck and moved closer. "Do you mind if I have a listen?"

Cruz struggled to sit up. "Sure."

While she listened to his chest and moved to his back, Cruz stared at Ford. Ford chewed his bottom lip, watching everything with worry etching his features. He didn't plan to leave. Cruz could deal with anything else, as long as Ford didn't leave.

Dr. Shannon draped her stethoscope over her shoulders again. "Well, all your tests came back great. I think it's possible you had a pretty severe panic attack. Have you been under a lot of stress?"

"Yes." There was no sense in lying.

"How many hours a day do you work?"

Ford snorted. "Twenty-four," he answered before Cruz could.

Cruz bristled. "It's not work if you love it."

Dr. Shannon cut in. "It's time to scale back. Stress can kill you as quick as a bullet. I'm recommending a few weeks off and you should call your doctor. While I didn't see any damage to your heart, your blood pressure was pretty high when they brought you in. That might be stress or you may need medicine to lower that number. Either way, you need to slow down. Take a break."

Cruz nodded, even though he had no intention of doing any of that.

"I'll make sure he follows your orders," Ford said, killing Cruz's plans to ignore all of this.

The doctor nodded. "Good. I'll get the paperwork started to get you out of here."

"Thanks," Cruz muttered. Now that he knew he

was fine; his brain was back to tackling the Ford issue. Ford wasn't moving. Cruz felt better, but then again, he didn't. He didn't want to go back to what they were before Ford decided to leave. Cruz wanted what they had become since.

Once they were alone, Ford moved back to his side. "I'm very much in love with you," Ford said, taking his hand. "I hope you know that."

Cruz had to take a breath as Ford's thumb stroked his knuckles. "I saw you with that guy." Cruz had to suck in another breath. "I'm sorry. My temper—"

"It's fine," Ford said, cutting him off. "You're a passionate person. Artistic temperament and all that."

Despite the laughter in Ford's voice, Cruz couldn't let it go. "I swear I don't mean to be such an ass, but somehow the worst side of me always comes out."

Ford kissed him, cutting off what was swiftly becoming another panic attack. "Stop," Ford whispered against his lips. Cruz took a breath. Ford's lips lightly brushed his. "I love you just as you are. In fact." Ford straightened away and dug through his pocket. He came out with a small box. "I made a stop before the casino tonight." He put the box in Cruz's hand and wrapped Cruz's fingers around it. "I'm staying in Vegas no matter what, but I'd like things to be different between us."

Cruz flipped open the box. His gaze moved from the gold band inside to Ford. Ford shifted nervously from one foot to the other. Cruz's curiosity doubled. "What's this?"

A smile exploded across Ford's face. "Please don't make me drop to one knee on this nasty emergency room floor."

Understanding dawned. "Are you asking me to marry you?"

"Not really." Disappointment slammed into Cruz before Ford wiped it away. "I'm telling you we're getting married. No more games or misunderstandings. We're supposed to be together, Cruz. Let's stop pretending things can be any other way."

"Okay."

"Seriously?"

Cruz spent a moment confused by Ford's reaction. "Of course, seriously. You're right. I don't want to go back to how we used to be, and you're mine. You can't be kissing other guys and shit, but I get that's my fault. I've let you think you're free, but you're not. You're mine." Cruz dragged out the words so there would be no misunderstandings. Ford belonged to him. Always had. Artistic temperament or just downright crazy, whatever his issue, Cruz would tear down the whole world if anyone came between them. Ford was his other half. "You should probably kiss me now."

Ford didn't hesitate giving Cruz exactly what he needed. They would be fine. In fact, they would be perfect. Cruz couldn't have it any other way. He had already almost lost Ford once. Losing himself wasn't far behind that scenario. Cruz would keep Ford happy. He would see.

EIGHT

Two weeks of rest was obvious hell for Cruz. In fact, Ford was fairly certain that Cruz had been sneaking around, working behind his back. He had caught Cruz on the phone with the shop a few times. Each time, Cruz would smile and claim it was nothing. He had just been checking in, making sure the guys were good. Ford always let it slide, because it was Cruz. Ford couldn't resist him, and Cruz was a workaholic. He had stayed in bed way more than Ford ever expected with very little argument. Ford couldn't complain.

The two weeks since Cruz left the hospital had been life-altering for both of them. Ford more so than Cruz. While Cruz hadn't been working, and that was a huge change for him, Ford was the one who had leapt from one life to another with both feet and no looking back. Cruz had refused to follow a single doctor's order until Ford married him. So they had married Vegas-style. No guests, drive-thru service, and cheap champagne had topped off the best day of Ford's life. Then Ford had quit his job to become a bigger part of Cruz's life. He was keeping things straight for Iconic while Cruz got some much-needed rest. While Ford suffered a lot of guilt over leaving his job when they had been so invested in him leading the new location in Phoenix, he had no regrets. This was the life he wanted.

"What are you doing?" Ford asked when he spotted Cruz putting on his shoes.

"Waiting on you so we can leave."

Ford glanced behind him. He had no idea what Cruz was talking about. Ford had been in the kitchen, drinking coffee just as he had been fifteen minutes earlier when Cruz had been in there with him. They had eaten breakfast together. Cruz hadn't said a word about them going anywhere. "Where are we going?"

The childlike smile Cruz wore when he was up to no good snapped to his lips. "It's a surprise."

Ford nearly groaned. Cruz and his surprises. Since they were married now, Ford had expected a certain level of Cruz returning to his old ways. Instead, he still kept going above and beyond for Ford. Instead of begging Cruz to tell him what was going on, he moved to get his shoes on as well. He didn't do it without an argument, though.

"No stress, right? You're supposed to be resting."

Cruz rolled his eyes. "How long do you plan to make me live like an invalid? I've spent two weeks behaving."

Ford met Cruz's stare. He no longer had to hide his heart. It was freeing in a way he couldn't describe. "I love you. I can't lose you. Just please don't rush right back into working yourself to death. Let me worry. Let me help."

Cruz stood and closed the distance between them. He didn't stop until he straddled Ford's lap. Cruz toyed with the ends of Ford's hair while holding his stare. "Baby, I'm not going anywhere. Not only do I refuse to leave you alone, there's no way in hell I can go back to not being glued to your side all hours of the day. No stress. We're in this together now."

With a nod, Ford conceded. He would trust Cruz to stay calm and alive. "Kiss me and then let's see this surprise."

Cruz moved slow, leaning in and capturing

Ford's mouth. Ford drew a steady breath. He swore love filled his lungs, sustaining him. Cruz was the absolute love of his life. Kissing him and touching him—hell, breathing him in—never got old. Cruz's health scare had given Ford a lot of perspective. There would never be enough years with Cruz to satisfy his heart. Ford had no clue how he had thought he could leave this behind.

For a moment, Cruz simply held Ford's bottom lip between his lips. He sucked. Ford gasped at the instant need that struck him from left field. An evil-sounding chuckle vibrated against his lips. "I know what you want, but you have to wait. Come on." Cruz sprang to his feet. The erection in Cruz's jeans couldn't be missed, but Cruz didn't seem to care. Ford drew a steady breath and stood. There was no sense in pouting. He would have Cruz later.

By the time they made it to the shop, Ford was somewhat cooled down. He was fairly confident he wouldn't embarrass himself anyhow. The hint of lingering desire he hadn't been able to shake disappeared at the sight of their destination.

"Your surprise is us going to work."

Cruz snorted. "It's not work if you love what you do."

Ford climbed from the truck and kept his smart-ass comments to himself.

Cruz waited at the front the truck. They linked fingers and walked inside together. Everyone rushed to the back of the shop at the sight of them, including Raiden, who Ford had only recently met. He didn't know why Raiden was there. It was a bit early for Jason's lunch break, but the pair had a hard time being apart. Ford was never surprised to see him, hanging around the shop and watching Jason work. Everyone loved him. Cruz and Ford followed the crowd to the back of the shop. Everyone was gathered around Jason's booth, filling the mouth and blocking the entrance.

"What's going on here?"

"You'll love it," Jason said, answering Ford's question with a non-answer.

Ford's gaze slid Cruz's way. "What will I love?"

Cruz wore his best naughty boy smile. "Well, the boys and I have been working on a special project. The boys more so than me, since I've been trapped in bed. I just finance things around here. Anyhow, when the guys helped move your stuff to my place, I had Eddie swipe your bike."

Goddamn. Ford had been so busy, he hadn't even noticed. "What did you do?"

Cruz held up his hands in surrender. "I didn't do anything I was in bed. But the guys, that's a different story. They just gave it a little makeover."

The guys cleared a path so Ford could see his Harley. His knees nearly collapsed. It was a work of art. Jason had transformed the paint job into a memorial for Ford's cousin. It was beautiful. Cruz blinked back tears. He had to turn away to gather himself. Every time he thought Cruz couldn't possibly outdo himself, he always found a way.

Ford forced himself to take a closer look at his bike. "Thank you guys so much. This is beautiful." His voice cracked and Cruz waved everyone away.

"Okay, everyone. Thanks for all your hard work. I think it's safe to say he loves it. Take the rest of the day off. I'm closing up early."

Ford swiped at his eyes on the down low as everybody cleared out, patting Ford on the shoulder as they passed. Once they were alone, Ford focused on Cruz. "I can't believe you did this. This is amazing. Really."

There was so much love in Cruz's expression, Ford wondered how he had ever missed it. He didn't understand how he had ever doubted Cruz. Cruz crowded his space. "I'd do anything for you. Truthfully, I've wanted to do this for more than two years, but I couldn't figure out how to snag the bike without you reporting it stolen. It was a hell of a lot easier now that we share a garage, but I still had to keep you from noticing."

Ford's throat was still so swollen, he had a hard time squeaking out words. He stroked Cruz's hair and jaw, wishing Cruz understood how beautiful he was in ways no one else knew. "I still can't believe I almost lost you."

Cruz turned his head and kissed Ford's hand before taking it between his. "I love you." Cruz looked exactly as he had while taking his wedding vows. Ford couldn't look away. "I know you don't care about monetary things and I could never buy you. Doing this for you was for me too, because sometimes I think my chest will explode without some outlet to show how much I feel for you." Cruz dropped his chin and stared at their clasped hands. "Before you almost moved away, I never told you how much I lived for talking to you every night. I never said a lot of things. Now we have the rest of our lives and it doesn't feel like enough time." Cruz winced as if he wasn't expressing himself well. "Forever wouldn't be long enough to satisfy me. I'm sorry. I'm not good with words."

"You're doing amazing." Ford shuffled closer. "I

think this is the first time we've ever been in this building completely alone."

Cruz pulled an exaggerated look of surprise. "You know, I think you're right. More to that, I don't know if you've noticed, but there's a really comfortable couch in my office."

"You don't say." Ford couldn't stop smiling. "Well, I've heard that newlyweds are known for their inability to keep their hands off each other, and I imagine we fit that bill."

Cruz's mouth lifted in one corner. "Then who are we to break with tradition."

"Exactly," Ford said, urging Cruz toward his office. Maybe they had been together long enough to be past this stage, but Ford loved touching Cruz. He couldn't imagine not wanting this gorgeous man who had given Ford a new last name. Maybe they could both be a little stubborn and dense, but they were meant to be. It was almost funny now. Ford had set out to start a whole new life just a few short weeks ago. Yet he had ended up with a completely unexpected future. Ford fully intended to embrace his new beginning. He couldn't have asked for a happier outcome. He couldn't have asked for a better life.

. . .

Keep an eye out for the next Messy Hearts, *Well-Played.*

Please consider clicking this link and leaving a review, https://www.amazon.com/review/create-review?asin=B0841RTFRL. Reviews really help with a book's visibility, which ensures I can continue writing. Thank you, Charity.

ABOUT THE AUTHOR

Charity Parkerson is an award winning and multi-published author with several companies. Born with no filter from her brain to her mouth, she decided to take this odd quirk and insert it in her characters.

*Eight-time Readers' Favorite Award Winner
    *2015 Passionate Plume Award Finalist
    *2013 Reviewers' Choice Award Winner
    *2012 ARRA Finalist for Favorite Paranormal Romance
    *Five-time winner of The Mistress of the Darkpath

Connect with her online:

—Sign up for my newsletter: http://bit.ly/CharityNews
    —Join my readers' group on Facebook: facebook.com/TeamCharityParkerson

—Website: charityparkerson.com
—Facebook:
facebook.com/authorCharityParkerson
facebook.com/TheMenofSin
—Twitter: twitter.com/CharityParkerso

www.ingramcontent.com/pod-product-compliance
Lightning Source LLC
Chambersburg PA
CBHW072230190626
46809CB00017B/1689